THE WRITING
RESILIENCE
ANTHOLOGY

THE WRITING RESILIENCE ANTHOLOGY

edited by Larissa Shmailo

MADHAT PRESS
CHESHIRE, MASSACHUSETTS

MadHat Press
MadHat Incorporated
PO Box 422, Cheshire, MA 01225

The Library of Congress has assigned
this edition a Control Number of
2024945190

ISBN 978-1-952335-87-7 (paperback)

Edited by Larissa Shmailo
Cover design by Marc Vincenz
Cover image: *Waterloo Bridge, Sun Through Fog* by Claude Monet, 1903

www.MadHat-Press.com

First Printing
Printed in the United States of America

*Dedicated to the participants
in the Writing Resilience Workshop*

Table of Contents

Introduction by Larissa Shmailo   xiii

Rachel Blum
For prompt, *What I said and what I should have said*   1
For prompt, *I obsess:*   3
For prompt, *Trust*   4
For prompt, *Trust*   5

Meg Tuite
Homemade Woman   7
Mummification   11
Hospice Care Suffers No Down Time   12

Sandra L. Kleven
Defiance Street: The Whole Damn Story   14
The Canny Invention   21

Susan Oringel
A Death of the Family   25
An Abecedary of Plenty   29

Claire Donohue Roof
Labor   32
Summer   33
My Fantasy Room   36

Elizabeth Morse
Kali's Clocks and Mirrors   38
Elevator Reign of Terror   42

Anna Fridlis
Black Hole   46

Audrey Roth
The Light of My Soul   54
Imogene!   58

Willian Considine
Being Bullied   63

Nina Glueckselig
Confessions of a Hoarder of Beauty   68
Julius the Dog   74

lisa roma
Starting with the Weather and the Ocean Doesn't Care   78
Between Heaven and Earth   80

Iris Gersh
Untangling My Father   82

Dennis Formento
It was insane, but ... just another night   89
Stones and Flowers   92

Paula Curci
You Know Her   97
Abbondanza!   99
Dysfunctional Timeline   102

Linda Kleinbub
I Promise Myself   105
Frigid   106
Victory at Vacation Day Camp   107

Andrea Nicki
Grandmother's Quilt   109
When We'll Worship Jesus   110
English Class 101   112

Cynthia Lee Steele
To Scream the Impossible Scream   114
Dancing Queen   119

Martha Kaplan

    Birth-days for baby boomers   124

    For Days of Auld Lang Syne   126

    Her Inner Child Loves the Wildness   128

    this empty page before me   129

    Across the Missouri Breaks   130

    Night rides on blue roads east of Austin   131

Larissa Shmailo

    Interview   132

    Fitness   135

    Madwoman   139

Contributor Biographies   143

Introduction
to *The Writing Resilience Anthology*

Dear Reader:

In the pages of this anthology, we invite you to embark on a journey of profound introspection, healing, and transformation. Writing Resilience is not just a collection of words; it is a testament to the power of the human spirit, a source of solace for those affected by trauma, addiction, and mental illness. Within these pages, you will encounter narratives that are at once creative and vulnerable, born from the depths of personal struggle and the triumph of resilience.

This anthology is a celebration of the writers who have taken part in the Writing Resilience workshop, where individuals bravely confront their past and present demons through the written word. Whether penned in the intimate setting of a workshop session or as a result of the thought-provoking prompts, the works you will discover here are the fruits of courage, catharsis, and creativity.

As you turn the pages of *The Writing Resilience Anthology*, may you be inspired by the courage of these writers and find, perhaps, a path to your own resilience within their words. This anthology is not just a collection of stories; it is a testament to the indomitable human spirit and the healing potential of the written word.

—*Larissa Shmailo*

RACHEL BLUM

For prompt, *what I said and what I should have said*

I said, *but the light is astonishing,*
and I think,
maybe I should have said more
about weeping

or how like rain light is—
a quiet animal face
mirroring the good, the saddest,
and mortality.

On his deathbed he said,
I really am not sure what is happening,
and I nodded

and now I'd like another chance
to sit and fail to say
what must not have been
important enough to say,

when instead I said,
I love you,
and was relieved
to have said
something true and simple,

the sky purpling over July
how it does.

For prompt, *I obsess:*

At the edge of the sea a voice repeats sentences
before repeating repetition—the head thinking
in languages with no word for *rest*. The way of rest
then, is to imagine a face, whereby language sees
it can rest, having reached its limits to conjure
a face.

*I am in one of the boats Reg built, smooth knees resting
on varnished ribs, so I imagine the inside of a polished whale.
Jim has returned from the dead, his alcoholic liver healed.
He joins his brother and lands the boat perfectly at the dock
on Indian Point. I know something about boats too, and tie
a nautical knot before climbing gracefully onto weathered
cedar. Jim says,* Have a look around, *and I reply,* Many bad things
happened here, but it has grown very beautiful. *The peninsula
appears in a way it never had—with magnificent flower
gardens, blossoming white, purple, and pink, and people
singing nearby. And beyond the choir, a pottery cottage
is nestled in tall grass, where people are making art.
On the dock, it is mid-ceremony—my daughter
about to be wed. Her groom wears a dark suit and black hat,
and she is dressed in white. It is a clear day. The sky is bright
blue and the surface of the lake bears a reflection of the world.
Jim is singing and remarks that in the time away, he learned
to sing.*

For prompt, *Trust:*

> God gives himself to men either as powerful
> or as perfect—it is for them to choose.
> —Simone Weil

the trust that we will pause
and look for Perfect Love
witnessing our broken world

and find a green
ring of light
supporting first syllables,

and rest there
while a particular
orchestra of birds

sounds out the window
this
sabbath morning.

face to face,
the residue of a nightmare
a breeze dispersed

as Love needs lovers
to want
for miracles.

For prompt, *Trust:*

bewildered,
looking into a grove
of willow and Christmas
trees,
lights strung among
like be-glowing air roots—

having tripped over natural grandeur
such as mountains
in the shapes of friends,
a train encompassing all history
and still—
the Arrivals board announcing,
ON TIME,
and a glimpse of sweet hair,
perfections of math
to a mathematician,
chemistry for a chemist,
a primal of nautilus,

an understanding of why
words you spoke at the very beginning
carried an atmosphere
we unnamed
until right there in the sea
was the diamond we had been looking for—

and you were inventing
a language
to help American English
contain
more words for love.

MEG TUITE

Homemade Woman

Frances clung to the hamhocks of a smack-mouthed infantry of a man and all the kitchen utensils for over fifty years. She baked pies, cakes, cookies, casseroles; broiled pork chops, steaks, turkeys, and bacon while his face and ass blew out the windows, the children, the TV.

Rose-scented and scrupulous, Frances handed out plates and heaped enough to keep neighbors, family, strangers from expecting anything more than a second or third helping from her with a nod.

Her husband's jaws were wrenches, screwdrivers, drill bits, shears, bottle-openers. They unhinged, turned, flipped, severed, chiseled, blasted foundations, and stifled oxygen.

Frances was fat with fear. A scale of winds battered inside begging her to look inward when she was disappearing, dissolving into the ether, bending as far away from herself until brittle enough to crack. A break was necessary to fit back inside herself so that she would be ready to die.

Her daughters were tired. The word 'mother' meant tedium, resignation, and headaches. Kids took on the flapping pages of a history that walked ahead of itself while Frances cleaned and cooked.

Her three daughters had skin that sloughed off the same page. Before they grew up they slumbered in single beds with wallpaper that cascaded some kind of Disney phantasmal parade of shackles. Beds were as perilous as depression. They gazed into their father's rumpled skin as often as the ceiling's scarred indents. Gnawing and gnashing, when they did sleep, had all of them in braces until their teeth grew together out of one prison. Without reprieve they turned inside out into seething teenagers. Frances succumbed to violence that radiated around the dinner table. Each forkful of chewed meat had Frances bloody with it. No one but the fat man had a volume dial turned full-throttle. He sawed and shoveled, squirted and seasoned. A homicide sat in every chair.

Fifty years of construction rattled through a lawnmown house. Disarray was laundered, swept out, scoured, and sanitized, yet nothing erased itself. Daughters with sons and daughters littered the background with their leaves of newly infected creepers. None of this brood had swallowed the slow salivation of days except Frances. Sweet nausea rose up in her throat when weight saddled around her stomach like another still-born. She didn't need a doctor to pull anything out of her this time. Viscous dark fluids clouded the toilet each morning. Frances was a weak floatation device. Today might be the day.

Instead, death startled her husband out of a sentence. His open-face turned into hot sauce as he choked on a shouting match with the muted TV. His team was losing and then silence sharpened the air between Frances and him. She limped from the kitchen to a body that hadn't even kicked back. She sat for what clocks could never decipher, and heard the staggering sounds of outside. Birds were whistling and a breeze made swishing sounds through the bushes. He was a strange portrait in his armchair. His legs and arms were splayed out and his slack face puzzled under open eyes that looked beyond the room as though he was listening too. The stain in the crotch of his pants was darkening with shit that belched the stench of rotted meat like the blast of one of those plug-in air fresheners through the room.

Frances picked up the phone and dialed. Her open-mawed mouth gurgled in what sounded more like a pot simmering than words.

"Mom?" a daughter asked.

"Dad," she said. Expectations were already lining up outside the door.

Most people resign themselves to blunted backdrops of landscapes they never notice until a sunset unhinges them. When silence clawed out of him, Frances witnessed the act of a body turning to stone as though this was the final curtain in a play.

The daughters came. They picked at invisible scabs. Frances washed his bloated body. They searched through the back of his closet until they discovered a suit that flared out on the hanger, but not on him. Frances carefully cut the back of the shirt, the suit-coat, and pants and slid them on him, one side at a time. The daughters moved his awkward, heavy limbs. Arms flopped and contorted without protest. One daughter said, "Oh God, sorry, Dad," when his head swung to the left. "His feet look cold," said the other and got some socks and struggled with his swollen ankles and toes that were already pooling blood underneath the skin.

"He's so quiet," said one.

"Serene," said the other.

"Remember how handsome he was, Mom?" one asked. She ran to find the photo albums.

Frances shook her head no. She was watching her own death scene and it was a rerun routed through their eyes. The swooping effect of shedding memories retired the dead mother of the pseudo-living and transported her from the artifice dicing onions, scraping bowls, forking piecrust edges, rolling dough, and stuffing carcasses into family and relatives. But he had beaten her even in sentiment.

"Can we keep the body overnight and call the funeral home tomorrow?" one asked. Frances covered his decaying body in rose spray, but his orifices were open caverns of festering ulcers and release. She cleaned the shit foaming out of his mouth and anus, but it kept coming. Nothing held back anymore.

"Just found Mom's recipe for apple crisp," one daughter yelled. Frances could hear her rummaging through cabinets in the kitchen.

"That was Dad's favorite," said the other with tears in her eyes.

"Can you make it for us, Mom?"

The man in the cut-up suit had a translucent sheen to his skin. The bruises matched his outfit, spreading opalesque storms up to the surface. Frances took his veined hands and folded them over each other. She could feel blood flooding between her legs. Today would be today soon enough.

Frances wasn't shaking anymore.

Mummification

Dolores, wedged between the fetid hosiery of skin and marriage, sinks into beige, unravels and plucks from an invigorating circulation. Damn if she isn't vertical as a dead marriage.

Lunacy of intrusion. Too much noise. Fragments scatter her. Diffuse outside terror. Unkempt choral clocks. Half-baked skies. Nights grope yesterdays. Hands circuit rooms. The uncle babysits. Her breath impotent. Uncle groans thunder. Bleary, overgrown carpet. That year hisses.

Dolores fractured being has been transparent, but becomes a shattered window of glass, her eyes a tragedy. Ten years of therapy tromp whatever glow she ignites on Tuesdays. Each pothole on the journey withers the poison of trust.

Middle child of middle America knuckles past legs until she is front and center. Moments when preparation is a misspelled task. A flask is bought in every state pissed in. Flasks flake dust in drawers all over the apartment. They wait to go somewhere. They go nowhere.

Sometimes Dolores smudges away days. Bottles ingest soft lips; batter with words. Woozy with the yawning edge of being is a sinking metaphor or just another particular loneliness that wraps its funk around the fibers of her sheets. She never invites anyone in.

Hospice Care Suffers No Down Time

Clouds rake across the sky, my pancreas. A Chinese doctor says my pulse is dry, white. An exact description of the only wine I buy and suck down every night. I stick out my tongue. He nods and writes down notes I don't care to decipher. He loads up a bag with tonics the color of dead leaves.

Everyone is dying in my daily life. I sit with a woman when an emerald green liquid starts to foam up from the depths of her. Her daughter and I put a flashlight down her throat and see it is thick and moving like lava up, up, up. We are captivated while her husband paces and roars in the background "WE TREAT OUR PETS BETTER THAN THIS".

His wife has been actively dying for weeks. She hasn't eaten. Her mouth plies open as I drip water and morphine into it. Every night is the last night. The daughter and I say goodbyes. Every morning she breathes and rasps, mammoth teeth exposed. The strength and girth of those incisors alone might keep her bound to this planet.

And, one day, as absurd as horror of routine, she dies. I lose a friend, another family, and a job.

And the clouds? Those warriors compliment sleep here in the desert where the sun stalks over 300 days a year. I am tired. The phone still rings. A number flashes across my screen from the house where the woman just died. Obliged to pick up, the familiar voices plead.

Turns out the husband wanted to die. His neighbors heard a gunshot at three in the morning and called the cops. He missed his heart by inches.

The chaplain asks if I can return, take care of him and his wound. Yes. It's an easy transition. I know the terrain. But now, he's not yelling.

He says, "I had a chance, and fucked it up."

I listen and work on cleaning and bandaging his wound. He wants to see my clouds.

"Maybe I should have called a vet," he says.

"Vets are more expensive," I say.

Sandra L. Kleven

Defiance Street:
The Whole Damn Story

*Last night as I was sleeping, I dreamt—marvelous error!—that
I had a beehive here inside my heart. And the golden bees were
making white combs and sweet honey from my old failures.*
—Antonio Machado

I want you to rise above Spokane.
—Theodore Roethke

*Inside you is an artist you don't know about....... Say yes quickly
as if you've known it from before the beginning of the universe.*
—Rumi

This explains my life.

I walk in poetry's mansion. Everything is shrouded with
sheets, from tables for toast to all things large. The sheets
themselves are shrouded on the shelf where they are stacked.

Down in the root cellar the celery in shrouded. What a
sight, this shrouded celery.

The sauna is shrouded; the sun porch, stairs, salon, the
situation, the sun, the sunset, the son, the sonic boom; the
sherbet and the sorbet.

The swimming pool is shrouded. Simple things are
shrouded. Sandra is shrouded. The shrouded are getting
crowded. Scimitars, slump, soot, saliva, sloths and the Soviets
are all shrouded.

Don't worry. This list is under control.

Everything in the universe that does not begin with the

letter S is also shrouded. All the shrouded objects, situations, jokes, epochs, passions, people (everything!) look like a gathering of common ghosts.

This is good. I am a poet. I have managed the universe with my mind.

Sandra was shrouded, a student of fiction. Anne Caston, a poet and faculty member, saw through it. Anne Caston's office was a vault, a windowless square. Anne Caston was the watchman. I brought her poetry—sheets of poems. I read them out loud. This went on for weeks. Then, she suggested that I abandon my fictional pursuit to join the poets. This had never occurred to me. Anne Caston said, "Come to the dark side."

So I did, though it meant stepping away from two book length manuscripts—a memoir and a novel—that drew me to the Creative Writing master's program.

In these long drafts, I recast catastrophes of Western Alaska to find some relief from things that bothered me. Most recent was a novel titled *The Story Thief.*

Before enrolling, I had been working on it daily for more than a year. As I closed in on 80,000 words, I had developed deeper questions about craft. To do the story justice, I needed professional help.

It was my ambition to move beyond the mainstream novel or memoir to coherently bring forth my quirky artistry. I wanted to locate the leading edge in craft and then exceed it. I was taken with the story I had created in *The Story Thief* and I realized that I could ruin it with clumsy writing. I entered the Creative Writing program at UAA seeking excellence so my skills could match the story.

But more important than this was a personal turning point reached in the fall of 2003. From that date, my intention has never varied. It was time to begin. I was not shiny and fit. I had no dress for the prom. Just show up naked, I told myself. If dresses are important, someone will make sure you get one.

That fall, I wrote many poems and thought they were good. I read them in the community. I introduced myself as a poet. But I turned to fiction, instead, and started to work on *The Story Thief*. I knew two poets when I was young—Ginsberg and Gluck—about as many poets as the world can bear. And if I did not think precisely this, I thought something close to it. It was one thing to write poems and how could a person *be* a poet? There is no work for poets. No money.

So, hoping to live from that time forward as a writer/artist, I dedicated myself to the novel. The follow correspondence written to a group of friends, on February 16, 2004, shows the certainty of this shift. I cannot improve on this description, found in the "groups" data-base at Yahoo:

> So how did I begin this recent spate of serious writing? It started, this recent fall, with feeling forcing word.... I heard Olinka Kalytiak Davis read.... She blazed a pretty little trail, broke through at least three limits I had unknowingly used to box myself in. She used the form for a presentation of self with all the troubles, dilemmas and delights that self contains ... but in new ways. Clever, abstract, layered, innovative. I saw this. Bought both books.

Begin to read at bedtime. Aloud. In part to keep sound and rhythm happening because then I'd wake up with lines and phrases. Needed at times a paper beside the bed to scribble what I didn't want to lose. Breaking rules that had restricted me..."Be brief" (As if everything was Haiku. As if the poetic "gift" was in taking the complex and abbreviating it.)

Drawing from Davis's collection, *Shattered Sonnets*, I offered the poem below as an example of her work (121).

One poem is about being interviewed. Since she is young (actually 40, but looks younger) and pretty, so gets discounted, no doubt.

> "To them you look just like a thirty-three (nine) year old woman. You are a thirty-three (nine) year old woman, with or without your strange husbandry: the quiet apiary out back, the seed packets of fallow.... When asked about youth admit that yours too has been wasted. When asked about beauty, admit that you have been asking too. When asked about truth, simply nod, yes."

This was the turning point, the launch, the crazed and dazzling drop into decadence and verse. The leaps within Davis's work broke into my mind ... creating fission or fusion, releasing phrases.

When I read her work my mind filled with other words that drew from my own dilemmas and drove me to the computer in the middle of the night.

Davis had also lived in Bethel—the frontier Alaska town that figures in my work. From *And Her Soul Out of Nothing*,

"Under the ice they are dragging the river...the ice will surely part and unveil the flushed body of the guy you heard of on the radio..."

One poem contains this concise line about the Eskimo language, Yupik, "... a language of long words made up of short words sewn together like pelts."

I learned from Davis that I did not have to be "rule bound." The sign of a rule sticking up like a stick in the middle of a line reveals an obedient poet—a good boy or girl. I had been a social worker for too long. I prefer the wild over here on the dark sigh. I mean, side.

Who wants to read one who is being good—that predictable transit—the risks all in the direction of proving the good of good, of God, and the Godly. Rules cool the rough dark of duende.

Here it is, from Franz Wright, "I dreamed I met William Burroughs,"

> I met William Burroughs in a dream.
> It was some sort of bohemian farmhouse,
> and he was enthroned, small and skeletal,
> in a truly gigantic red armchair.
>
> When I asked him how he was, he replied
> Well, you know what they say—for best results,
> always mock and frighten lobster before boiling.
> Franz—I like that name, Franz. Childe Franz
>
> to the dark tower something or other … Hey,
> got a smoke? And quit worrying so much:
> they can't help themselves, they're like abused dogs
> and they're going to react to affection and kindness
>
> with uncontrollable savagery. Just tell them,
> You're out of my mind, pal. You're out
> of my mind. Either that or, I'm out of yours.
> That'll keep them brain-chained to their trees.

Writing then, in Bethel, Alaska, I thought my work was good, but I was alone—alone with wonderful friends who were as supportive as friends can be, but I didn't know where the work stood in the scheme of things. It occurred to me that I could be a world-class poet—whatever that was. No one in my range of daily living was a reliable judge. Still, I had a hunch. I told a friend that the eventual publication of my poems was a foregone conclusion.

Nonetheless, I focused on the novel instead of poetry because I saw no vocation as a poet. How would I live—even if this music were enduring? Material for the novel surfaced. I wrote poetry but all my focus was *The Story Thief*.

Graduate school was a near fiasco. I was not fully welcomed. This perplexed me. I dropped my first class and came close to leaving the program. My commitment helped me hang on though, still naked, in need of a dress.

In time, I saw I had wandered into the fallout of old disputes within the department that had nothing to do with me. In time, the distortions gave way and I was able to go on. Sometimes I think it was a necessary test.

"Circus, My Circus," which appears early in my collection speaks to the shift from one circus to another, as a social worker arriving here. The speaker asserts "self as artist," while looking balefully at the new performers, where the clowns were just like "the ones I know." Still a student of fiction, when I wrote it, I begin to see how the short form could serve my need to frame experience.

When I stepped officially into poetry's cauldron, I told Anne Caston the following story: In 1976, my aunt, who happens to be seven years younger than me, had a poem accepted for publication.

In a mix of admiration and jealousy, I told myself that I would write a poem that very day—and it would be published. If she could, I could. So I did. "Northwest Reverie" was a poem about the death of Mark Tobey. Not long afterwards, the poem won in a competition sponsored by the local paper and published in a special "Writer's Edition" of the *Bellingham Herald*. Encouraged, I wrote another. Eventually, there were four poems.

I finished my bachelor's degree in Human Services and I begin writing in conjunction with my work. I wrote grants and I wrote material for a theatre company with a focus on preventing child abuse. Saved the four poems in a file; my life's work.

When I told this to Anne Caston she joked about my four-poem canon. I had not understood that a poet might write constantly or that a lifetime of work might result in hundreds or, possibly, thousands of poems. I did not grasp that the flow of acceptance and rejection was a constant—no reflection on the work—just the way it works. I would eventually see that submission of poems must be as much a routine as tooth-brushing or bathing.

The Canny Invention

In order to write a poem, you have to invent a poet to write it.
—Antonio Machado.

I enter my last decades. In diminishing moments, in the vanishing, I call myself poet and begin the canny invention.

Sandra, remember who you are. You have roots with the beats, the hip, the absurdists, Albee, Beckett, Ionesco, Genet. You got your kicks on Route 66. You read Burroughs' *Naked Lunch* while in high school, skimmed it, anyway, for the nasty parts in that incoherent logarithm of junk and jissom. You read Norman Mailer, Lawrence Durrell, and Paul Krassner's *The Realist.*

All of this material from that Harvard boy. Let's call him Charlie. You found this reading intoxicating. Forbidden—and a contrast to the bland sprawl of conformity out beyond Seattle's north end. You spoke then about the felt yoke of conformity. In the spring of your junior year, you had had it with the "rah, rah" of high school. You read Beckett's *The Unnamable,* memorizing this part:

> "Whether all grow black or all grow bright, or all remains grey, it is grey we need to begin with, because of what it is, and of what it can do, made of bright and black, able to shed the former or the latter and be the former and latter alone. But perhaps I am the prey on the subject of grey, in the grey, to delusions."

Why? Not because you thought it was profound. It was because of the strained convolution and way the final sentence undermined the entire edifice.

21

Four months from graduation, you were sent home from school because the administration learned that you were pregnant. They wanted you gone like an infection. You had no heart for a fight. It was better to go and find better people somewhere. You looked for them in the University District with Charlie. You found something there. The dark time became good time.

The Blue Moon tavern in the University District was the center of a social milieu that included professors, poets, Marxists, artists and alcoholics. There was an ethic of inclusion and no one passed judgment except against the squares.

These lines from Louise Bogan's "Several Voices out of a Cloud" capture this veneration of the underside, distain for the good citizens.

> Come perverts and drug takers; come perverts unnerved!
> Receive the laurel, given though late, on merit; to whom and wherever deserved.
> Parochial punks, trimmers, nice people, joiners, true blue
> Get the hell out of the way of the laurel. It is deathless and it isn't for you.

Theodore Roethke taught at the University of Washington and he drank at the Moon. In winter of 2010, as part of my MFA degree I went back to the University District to make a film about Roethke—an homage. It was a homecoming. When I arrived in the district, expelled from high school, I was too young to drink at the Blue Moon Tavern but I moved among those who were Roethke's friend. Soon I had a baby and didn't do night life. I was busy trying to finish high school. But I knew this community—when my high school pushed me out, these wild ones embraced me—made me feel like I was on the leading edge of cool. That's nice at eighteen.

Do you remember now? You and Charlie went to North Beach, met Ferlinghetti. Later, Bob Dylan was the one you believed in. You did some acid. Pot made you paranoid and twice put you into five minutes of white blindness. You shot up once to be able to say you tried it. You did. It was amphetamine. You are such a confessor.

Liked speed (in tablet form) but avoided it because the amphetamine junkies were dying. Sandra, you hate to be judged. You wanted to sleep around and did your best, but it was hard to be so free.

Hear this now. You know about this. How there is work and the work's work. Something you chew in the swamp of your mouth. You know that taste—honey and bile. You swallow it whole. You are always the last to know who you have failed. If you are to end your life without a sense of failure, it will be because, outside of your ramblings, this other half digested thing has come up again as swell vomit, well formed, refined. You close your eyes, blue and black mingle. Your fancy is tickled.

Roethke says, "None the less, in spite of all the muck and welter, the dark and the dreck of these poems, I count myself among the happy poets."

There are things words cannot express but there is a name for everything—Bruce, Brighton, Belinda. There is a forest leopard whose eyes shoot gold killing beams. You slide under it with your slippery language because Adam could name things. You can name your childhood, Blithe. You can name the Johnson administration Butch. Blithe and Butch might mingle. It was a debauchery followed by blight. You can change the names, the mingling, the monstrosity, the romance. Open a vein and bleed.

The minions gather like ants. Take a stick and poke at the dirt where they enter underground chambers. You have done this in the past. There are names for girls like you.

I embraced a different morality, one of kindness and compassion, where one does not pick fights, does not judge others until the evidence of wrong is overwhelming, one that was not much concerned with who you slept with and why. In the morality to which I ascribe, killing is to be avoided, and rich and rewarding sexual expression is a virtue. A relationship's requirements for fidelity are arrived at mutually, not through enforced social norms.

I woke up today with the idea of shrouding. It is in keeping with the process of discovery. The reach of the metaphor is magnificent, as when Sylvia Plath spanned the United State with "Daddy":

> Ghastly statue with one gray toe
> Big as a Frisco seal.
> And a head in the freakish Atlantic.
> Where it pours bean green over blue.

Beat the batter for a bunt cake. She was one battered babe. Did the batter bunt? The possibility was pleasing. A penchant for paradox among the gadflies and the limned Godfreys of regret. Reckless assembling wreaks havoc on a line—epochs end with the tattering fingers of the poet.

Susan Oringel

A Death of the Family

It was insane, but I thought I could fly out to Denver in August 2007 to my dying mother a few weeks before the end and help her have a "good death." Though the odds of helping someone with whom I'd had a very rocky relationship seemed low. I'd been able to help some of my most difficult clients find healing through deep listening and reflecting back their feelings. Surely, I could do some of that with my mother.

It was insane to believe my physician friends who said dying of a brain tumor would be an easy death: she'd just get sleepier and then pass. No, the more debilitated she got, the more agitated she became because she was terrified of not being in control. And of death. I could understand that, but I was anguished I couldn't find a way to help her.

It was absolutely insane to equate being with my mother to working with clients. I hadn't grown up with my clients and I was never dependent on them as a child. But I wanted at the end to have the deep talks I never had with my mother. I hoped this one time we could be honest with each other (as we had rarely been), but we never got there. Actually, in those final days I saw my mother become more "herself," angrier, more frightened, and even less willing to admit needing, or to ask for, help.

But I did get gifts from those final weeks. A mother and daughter working for the home health agency that my sister had hired had really bonded with my mother and wanted to be there 24/7 in her final days. Harla was nearer my mother's age and Dee Ann closer to mine. They were both born-agains—which frightened me at first—but they were respectful and just wanted to help my mother "transition" (a word common to end-of-life parlance). They ended up being more helpful to me.

When my mother would tantrum and scream and I would relive being a scared five-year-old, DeeAnn would put her hand on my back and say, "Don't dissociate—this is not about you." She had had some counseling training, bless her! Which made me marvel about the unlikeliness, as well as the gift of having a trained witness at my side.

And when I borrowed my mother's car while she was sleeping, to meet my sister and brother-in-law for dinner, I was later met at the front door by Harla, who whispered Mom was mad because I'd taken the car without asking. Was I supposed to have awakened her? Suddenly I was 17 again.

And so it went day after day, my mother, the former esteemed history teacher, getting more and more upset and making less and less sense. "You think I'm stupid," she'd say, and I'd reply, at times with more compassion than others, "No, Mom, I think you have a brain tumor."

She had been terrified my sister would send her to a nursing home, so my sister—for once—was the one banished from the house. It felt strange not to be the black sheep of the family. But what a gift to realize that being the "favorite" wasn't much better than being an outcast.

It was insane, but almost ten years to the day of my mother's death, my sister accused me of stealing Mom's stuff, especially her jewelry, which my sister had declared she wanted no part of. Mom's over-the-top gold items fit neither of our styles, but I urged her to at least take the unmatched left-overs so that she could sell the gold. Later she found those leftovers proof that I was cheating her.

Believing I had cheated her was especially ironic because my mother kept confusing my sister with her own mother— whom she resented deeply—and had wanted to take my sister out of her will. My mother kept her in, only because I begged her to, saying, "Mom, I want to have a relationship with Patti after you're gone."

But after my sister's accusations and my sending her all the items she wanted—from an itemized list she demanded I provide—we have exchanged a few emails—my cancer, her third marriage, my first—but we are basically not speaking.

The last day of my mother's life began with a loud bang coming from my mother's bedroom. I jumped up from the sleeper couch in the living room and ran into my mother's room to find her crawling on her bedroom rug. It was five a.m. and she had fallen on the way back from her bathroom. It was also the birthday of my partner Don, who had died suddenly five years earlier. Dee Ann came running in from my father's old bedroom, soon after. My mother would not let us help her get up: she was afraid we'd drop her. So, we hung out, us standing, my mother sitting on the floor. "Bev, do you want some coffee?" Dee Ann offered and came back with a mug. And that's how time passed for a few hours. My mother finally crawled to the bed, and only when we *promised* to drape her over it, and lift her legs, did she let us get her back in bed. I marveled at the intensity and insanity of her insisting on being in total control and at how futile it was—and that she missed a chance to feel loved and cared for; she missed a chance to be helped. I promised myself to remember this.

My mom moaned and dozed after the ordeal. Later an overnight nurse from Hospice showed up and we both sat in my mother's room, talking softly. We introduced ourselves to each other and I remember she talked about getting out of a terrible marriage and I mentioned Don's death. And how he was the first man I really trusted and how hard it was to lose him.

My mother's moaning increased. I walked over to the side of her bed and placed my hand as gently as I could on her hair and stroked it softly. With all the force my mother could muster she threw my hand off her hair as if some loathsome insect had just assaulted her. In shock, before I could stop myself, I said, "Fuck you!" And I honestly don't know what happened after that. At some point I was back in the room talking to the nurse. And then my mother's breathing changed. I remarked on it and the nurse agreed. Softer, less fitful. I went to the side of her bed and listened—and she was gone. It was 11:45 p.m., the last fifteen minutes of Don's birthday.

The funeral home came at 2 a.m. with a hearse to take my mother's body away. I read "When Death Comes" by Mary Oliver at the funeral and choked up at "I was a bride married to amazement / I was the bridegroom taking the world into my arms" because these things were also true about my mother. But that is another story.

An Abecedary of Plenty
for Audrey Roth

Abundance: a field of yellow sunflowers, heads nodding in the sun

Affluence: a pantry stocked with fresh spices, oils, grains and beans

Beauty: the shocking red of a male cardinal in the dead of black-white winter

Comfort: down duvet over flannel sheets on a cold night with my beloved bed mate

Copiousness: embarrassment of riches, effusion and excess, lovely muchness, floods and falls of never-ending crimson flowing from a cup

Deliciousness: fresh pesto blended from the garden with just-picked tomatoes, hot cinnamon spice tea with soymilk in a handmade mug

Direction: that subtle inner map that has carried me throughout my life in explorations of heart and mind, that has led me to writing, teaching, counseling, and expressing Spirit from a body

Enveloping: the skies of the Midwest and Southwest, stretching for miles with almost palpable clouds

Equanimity: being able to sail the seas of change in every moment, feeling guided by the breath of Spirit

Freedom: swaying on the winds of thought but not being bound, lying in a hammock that swings with the breezes, days filled more with appreciation than chores

Fortune: a writer's shack on a beach or lake, wintering in Florida, Mexico, or the Caribbean, a house overlooking water, good books published and the time to write more, more years with my husband and deepening closeness, a healthy body that weathers the changes of aging, a stronger, warmer connection with Creation and the Divine

Gratitude: for gifts given, a fertile mind, a body that can move and stretch even with the limits of aging, good friends who mirror who I am, my cats-little spirit-beings, also mirrors

Happiness: knowing both sun and rain are both necessary for growing

Insight: in words, in dreams, in the body, those sudden flashes of knowing

Joy: letting what I have be more important than what I don't have

Knowledge: appreciation for what I have learned while opening myself to more

Love: like the energy of the sun, makes every good thing grow

Landscape: the red rocks of Utah carved by God, the rolling cold ocean of Maine, Iowa's fertile fields, the gardens, plants and trees of my yard, all enlivening, providing pleasure

Merriment: jokes and laughter, a shining between souls

Now: the only time I have

Openness: letting the all-loving goodness of God pour into me

Prayer: asking for what I want but also aligning with the will of Spirit

Quiet: the fertile center from which comes all creation

Rest: nourishment and rebuilding of body and soul

Safety: dwelling in the arms of God, now and forever

Trust: knowing in body and mind that I am safe

Travel: back to the islands of Greece, to the Holy Lands, back to India, to Paris with Mark, to Hawaii, to get to know Mexico, learn to speak Spanish fluently again, to visit my good friends all over the world

Unchain: to free myself from all actions and thoughts that no longer serve me

Valor: grit, spirit, courage to meet life on life's terms

Wisdom: to keep learning what I came here to learn in a body

Xylophone: to be the bright instrument God plays through,

Yield: may I surrender to life AND also bring forth, bear and blossom

Zeal: may I be filled with enthusiasm and joy forever.

Emeth. Amen.

CLAIRE DONOHUE ROOF

Labor

I gave birth to four babies in galaxy pain, muscles stretching
     far into Never, Never Land....
I felt the ocean holding my breath as a hostage.

Take these four rubies of my heart box beating.
Make these battles of hope and division let us all live.
Fly my prayers like summer kites into the robin blue sky.

Doctors' voices are babbling into my midnight dreamsicle
     contractions.
I remember summer, winter, autumn, and spring sex and love
     that created these sharp spirits.
The pregnancies connecting membranes of eyelashes,
     eardrums, lips and lungs ...

I hear Joni Mitchell's *Blue* album songs in my head.
I see Natalie Wood's beautifully doomed movies when I close
     my eyes.
The nights of nine months four times over take me to some
     empire ecstasy.

All I have now are lungs on fire.
At their births, I breathe emeralds.
I have worked the clay into the bones of them.

Summer

It was summer, 1968. I was nine years old. The three Donohue sisters, Mary, Claire, and Ann were spending a few weeks with our Grandma Cora at her house in Coldwater, Ohio. I remember sitting on her small back porch where she taught me how to shell green peas from her garden. I learned how to sit and snap fresh green beans. Grandma Cora usually got up around 5:00 am and make little breakfast. Little breakfast was usually her coffee, toast with jam, and a bit of bacon. Then, around 9:00 a.m., she would make big breakfast. There were fresh eggs, more bacon, more toast and homemade jam, and American fries. There were also little boxes of cereal that we kids could choose from. Milk was fresh in glass container, with the cream rising to the top of the jar.

"Mom," my mother would say, "the kids are not going out to work in the fields!" There was such a spread on the dining room table. We kids loved all of it. Grandma Cora creamed all of the vegetables with a combination of flour, spices, butter, and milk. In the evening, she would pop homegrown popcorn in bacon grease and then salt the popped corn.

One morning, it was still dark outside the house when Grandma woke us up. My two brothers, Joe and Danny, and my Uncle Bob had gone fishing early that morning. We girls, still in our summer nightgowns, followed my Grandma Cora into the kitchen. The kitchen was small. There was newspaper spread on the wood kitchen top. My eyes and nose came right above the tabletop.

Grandma Cora said, "This is how you skin a catfish." Then, she slapped a big wet catfish onto the newspaper. *Whap!* She chopped off the fish head. *Whomp!* She chopped off the tail. It was at this moment that I made my prayer to God. "Please, God, let me learn how to do some kind of job where I don't have to skin a catfish!" The fish had sharp teeth and spine. I continued my prayer over and over while she tugged at that fish.

Eventually, the fish was cleaned, and dropped onto some corn meal Then, she fried it in a big black pan that had hot oil popping from it. There were other fish that she cleaned and fried for us that morning. I just got pale and felt like fainting. I knew how to say Hail Mary's, and Our Father prayers. Yet, in that moment, I had made my own prayer and my own goal, not a prepared prayer or a goal that grown-ups wanted for me. It was just me and God. My plea and my focus.

I would repeat a version of that prayer to God whenever Grandma Cora determined my sisters and I needed to know how to kill, pluck, and make a chicken for dinner. Grandma could also tell us how to butcher a hog. For that, one needed a big family to help. Grandma had to know all of these skills and more to keep herself and her family alive. I grew up and became an English teacher. I think that moment she chopped off the head of that catfish, it was clear my path was elsewhere.

Light at the end of the tunnel …

At dusk, at Grandma and Grandpa Reichert's house, we grandchildren would gather fireflies in their backyard/garden. The fireflies, or lightning bugs, would hover over the asparagus garden. By August, the asparagus had gone to seed, spreading out in bushes. My sisters and brothers, and any cousins visiting also would catch the fireflies in mason jars. We kids would punch holes in the jar lids. In their town of Coldwater, there was a swamp behind Grandma and Grandpa's alley. The late summer sky would be filled with starlight and the light from hundreds of fireflies. My brothers would sometimes open the jars in my grandparents' house. We would all watch the lightning bugs scatter throughout the two-story white house. The whole house would glimmer as summer came to a close.

My Fantasy Room

There are birds of paradise that fly around my fantasy. Altars to the goddesses and to Mother Mary grace the room. All the lovers that I have truly loved dance the samba with me. My hips move to the beat of music always playing on my throwback record player. Penelope Cruz teaches me the art of the beguiling smile, and Ntozake types up our next visit to a dance hall that is a secret to the world.

Apricots and baklava are on the table with the white lace tablecloth. And when my invited guests are hungry, Frankie's Barbecue appears at the lilac front door. Catherine, Rachael, Natalia, and Zachary are dressed to the nines for the holidays. They play hopscotch and basketball depending on the weather. When thunderstorms arrive, there are no tornadoes, only electric blue skies turning wildly grey with dazzling lightning show.

My four siblings fall from heaven all young and dear again. Our mother, our queen, our Demeter, our hearts desire, appears in a caftan of many colors. She brings her French perfume. We read recipes from heaven and my kitchen is full of fresh fruit and the most modern gas stove. The radio is telling us all the news from a parallel universe, where people read their own Amazon jungle for clues on how to live. Here, at my fantasy, there are always the just perfect hair products for every woman. Everyone makes a fair wage. Limousines are available to take my guests and me to art museums. We stop off at women's shelters and shower the place with protective prayers and spells.

This room, filled with books about women artists and stunning black and white photographs of my childhood fill the walls. When it snows outside, there are purple irises in that yellow vase we love so much. No one is too cold or too hot. Young and old are beloved beyond what is called for in advice columns. There are not itchy tags on any of our clothes. People come and go with Polaroids of the parties we have had. Coffee is made with dark beans picked not by children. We always have sweet cream and warm mittens. No men throw their shoes at their children here. Poverty goes away and there are no kings to please.

Typewriters appear on tables at just the right times. Paper comes in many colors, and all the art supplies dazzle the visitors who have been in prison unjustly. We sing Motown songs until we cannot breathe. Prince brings us his guitars and admires the gardens out the wide windows of my space.

There are women who cover their hair and women who do not. All are embraced and offered hot or sweet tea. There are enough bedrooms for people to stay overnight if they wish. Clean linen sheets are covered with homemade quilts that teach people how to escape slavery. And at the end of the days, there is my favorite love, waiting with his long lean legs and strong hands, holding out to me a signal that it is a good time to turn off the lights. In the shadows, I think I see the silhouettes of Octavia Butler and Ursula LeGuin. There is a wrinkle in time here now, and I am willing to go there time after time.

ELIZABETH MORSE

Kali's Clocks and Mirrors

Her name was Kali after the mother goddess who destroys evil to protect the innocent. The Kali I knew wasn't so aggressive, but she did protect me. Like her namesake, she was from India, but spent a tame childhood in the UK.

When I met her, she ran an antique shop. It was 1967. The store was tiny, but it contained treasures.

One January day, I wandered over to the window after school. I was in no hurry to get home. My mother would be passed out on the couch while burning meat she was serving for supper. Or she might be irate, accusing me of taking something of hers. Neither of these possibilities was appealing.

In the window, the antique shop had a mirror. Despite greasy hair and chubby cheeks, my reflection didn't look half-bad.

I pushed open the door. Might as well have a look around at all the fascinating objects. I had plenty of time until the bus pulled up.

A bell rang as soon as I stepped inside, and a woman sitting in a rocking chair looked up. "Are you looking for anything in particular?" she asked.

Yes, but it wasn't in any of those blue glass bottles with shapely stoppers. I was looking for what some girls in my class had, the ones who often spoke in class and were cheerleaders. I was looking for a way to grow into my own life.

I shook my head and started wandering around. She went back to her knitting, which I noticed went more quickly than my mother's. Or my own, for that matter.

She wore a magenta silk scarf that covered most of her hair, which was parted in the middle and punctuated with a few strands of gray. An oversized fisherman sweater hung from her shoulders, covering most of a straight skirt. She had on dark tights and loafers.

Clocks hung on every wall, few of them operational. They were stopped at the times I started a novel I loved, did a sketch, made fudge or wrote a story: moments to savor. There were also mirrors with frames ranging from simple to ornate. Before long, I was seated in the armchair opposite her, describing how my mother screamed that I'd have to work in Woolworth's if I didn't get better grades. I talked about my friend Yvonne and the books I was reading.

She listened. Then, she stood up and gestured toward my reflection in the mirror and said, "You're beautiful! You have everything to look forward to." She was just being kind, but her words felt better than any I'd heard in a long time.

Then, finally, she said "You're going to outgrow all of this, and your life will improve."

No one had ever told me that.

The next time, I brought Yvonne, the friend my mother liked best. "We'll just stop in for a moment," I said, as we left school. "It's on your way to the train station."

"If you insist, Annie," she said. I'd asked her to call me Anne, but she called me Annie anyway.

The bell rang and Kali smiled. She made us tea in dainty cups from a hot plate in the back.

Yvonne pulled her coat closer around her shoulders. She shook out her hair and said she had to go; she had an exam to study for.

Once we were outdoors, she said, "You really like all that old stuff? How do you even know those cups are clean?" She wrinkled her nose and hurried off into the evening.

Maybe Yvonne was right. I didn't go back for a few weeks.

Right after a peculiarly painful day at school, one in which I'd been awarded a D+ on a math notebook, I stopped by the shop. Today Kali was wearing a green silk scarf to cover her hair. We talked. Finally, she said, "You'll be an artist if that's what you want to be." As I left, I felt much better.

Although my parents spoke sharply, they were comfortable with my poor grades. I was probably more upset than they were. Academic excellence was my mother's bailiwick. She was a professor of American history and proud of her PhD. Her self-deprecating humor and constant complaints about her weight told me that the academic world was all she believed she had.

I stopped in often. Spring came, and my cheeks were a little less chubby and my hair a little less greasy. For the first time, I made the honor roll.

I finally told my mother why I was often home late. Then she insisted on meeting Kali.

In hindsight, I understood why she might want to do that. Kali was, after all, a stranger.

My mother and I went to the shop on a Saturday. When we pushed in the door, Kali got up and shook my mother's hand, which was held out stiffly in greeting. My mother refused tea but ate Milano cookies. She seemed anxious, the way she had when I'd watched her teach.

Afterwards, my mother never gave me grief about my visits. She knew she was beaten. Empathizing with her daughter was more than she could bear and best left to someone else. Her own mother just criticized her weight and praised her academic accomplishments.

After Kali sold the shop, I went to visit her apartment across town. It had tiny rooms, as well as ancient plumbing. The antiques, including a dressmaker's dummy, a grandfather clock and the mirrors, had migrated there. She taught me to knit quickly and inattentively, the way she did.

She told me about her life. Her husband, who died way before I met her, had survived the holocaust. She showed me a photo of a man with blond wavy hair and round glasses. They had met in an orchestra where she played cello and he played piano.

By junior year, I was making the same grades my mother had. I'd found ways to make my daydreaming self-focus. Kali was proud of me.

"When I was your age, grades meant something!" my mother fumed, perusing my report card. "Now, there's been a grade rise and grades mean nothing!"

After that I realized she wasn't the one I was working so hard for. I was growing into my own life.

Before I left for college, Kali gave me an old raccoon coat. It had a houndstooth wool lining, sewn by her, but there were still a few holes between the pelts. "You need to mend it with fishing line," she said. "Go to a sporting goods store. Then use a fur needle." The raccoon pelts were tough, but I followed her instructions. So I had a warm coat for those Hudson Valley winters, all four of them.

I wish I had stayed in touch. Was I too wound up in trying to reinvent myself? After I moved out of the last dorm, I never returned to live with my parents.

But I often thought of the grandfather clock, the one built to track the tides; the dressmaker's dummy that was in the size both Kali and I wore; and the carrot cake we baked. Then there were all those glorious and dependable mirrors.

Elevator Reign of Terror

When I was in my teens, I developed a phobia of riding in elevators, especially when I went alone. This fear just came over me one day, and I hesitated to step into an elevator in the building where I lived with my parents. I must have stood there in the lobby for at least five minutes. I realized that I did have to go home to my room where I could listen to the radio and read. Otherwise, I'd miss dinner. If I stayed long enough, I'd miss Alison Steele, the night bird, disk jockey of the wee hours on WNEW-FM.

With trepidation, I stepped inside the elevator car. The door slid shut, and I noticed a graffito on the wall: PEOPLE GET READY, THE ELEVATOR IS DROPPING. Just what I needed.

As the elevator clicked off floors up to the twelfth where I lived, I held my breath. Finally, the doors loosened and sprang apart, as did my fear. Now, I could go home.

A few years earlier, I had been raped and mugged in these same elevators. When I was eleven, I stepped inside with a male teenager. He was wearing a tan jacket that was typical for that year, 1965. He pressed the button for the floor just below mine. I didn't think anything of it.

When we stopped at his floor, he pointed a switchblade at my neck. Then he dragged me out and into the concrete-walled stairwell, promising to kill me if I screamed. Once there, he proceeded to rape me, an overweight eleven-year-old girl in a shapeless corduroy jumper and turtleneck shirt. He pulled my dress up and my underwear down.

Finally, I started to cry. He pulled the knife away and let me go. "Don't tell anybody," he said.

Once I was home, I informed my mother immediately. The police came and asked me explicit questions about the boy's anatomy, which made me fidget in my chair. He was never caught. Got to love the NYPD of the mid-1960s.

Later that evening, I couldn't stop throwing up.

The mugging was a couple of years later. Mercifully, it took less time and didn't involve bodily fluids. Again, I got into the elevator with a lone male. All I remember about him was that he was wearing a longish camel-colored coat.

As soon as the elevator arrived at my floor, he stuck his foot into the door to prevent it from opening. "Give me your money!" he demanded.

I opened my wallet in a panic. Change rained down into the floor. I had to pick up each and every penny, nickel, dime and quarter while this guy towered over me, just watching.

After I handed it over, he let me go.

Once again, the police were called. At least they did not make me uncomfortable with explicit questions. They never caught the guy this time, either.

About a year later, my elevator terror began. When I went out, I waited for an elevator that had two or more people in it because I felt safer that way. I did the same when I came home.

I often dreamt of stepping into elevators with no floors, or those with floors that dropped out halfway through the ride. I dreamt of elevators stuck for days in interminable dark shafts and elevators crashing and breaking every bone in my body.

Of course, all of this posed more problems than I imagined at first. New York is a vertical city after all, proud of its skyscrapers like the Empire State and Chrysler buildings.

What was I going to do? Never mind visiting friends; I had to get a summer job. And this despite my mother's complaints that I had what she referred to as emotional problems and would almost certainly never work.

The situation was just not acceptable. My parents were screaming drunks. My father bashed my head into a wall and threatened to knock me down every so often. I had to get out. I had to get my own place as soon as I graduated from college. And what I'd need to do that was the ability to hold a job.

I tried the local stores and restaurants for summer work but had no luck. The temp agencies offered employment answering phones, but to get it, I'd have to go downtown or midtown and ride an elevator to a floor with a frighteningly high number. The World Trade Center Towers were new, and there were lots of jobs there.

I couldn't tell anyone about my fear. Unfortunately, my father had seen me panic when elevator doors failed to open while the car moved up and down without stopping until we rang for help. He'd screamed at me, so no one else could know. Not even a therapist or psychiatrist.

Looking for an office job was just trouble. At first, I stood motionless in skyscraper lobbies. I wasn't about to step into any of these elevators alone.

Then I had it figured out. I would only ride elevators when the crowds were there: (1) 8:00 a.m., 8:30 a.m., 9:00 a.m., 9:30 a.m. for arrivals, (2) 12:00 noon, 12:30 p.m. and 1:00 p.m. for lunch, and (3) 4:30 p.m., 5:00 p.m., and 5:30 p.m. for departures. If many people were in the elevator with me, I'd be relatively safe. I also told myself repeatedly that hordes of people rode elevators every day and weren't maimed or killed.

The good news was that I was going to be able to work. I was going to be able to live independently.

So I've been working in skyscrapers in Manhattan and Jersey City for over forty years. I even worked on the fiftieth floor of one of the World Trade Towers during the 1980s. I'm no longer terrified, just a tad nervous. Once I volunteered to ride the elevator with someone else who was afraid, someone my co-workers laughed at. But I got it.

I can go alone now. It's not much of an issue. What a relief!

I must admit that when I drank, I felt no fear in elevators. Unfortunately, my phobia fueled my alcoholism.

Fortunately, the fear stayed away after I got sober. While not completely terror-free, I visit friends and work in high-rise offices with impunity. No big deal.

Anna Fridlis

Black Hole

I started my summer break with a bright hope for my fall sabbatical from university teaching: to draft a significant chunk of the memoir I haven't been writing for the last seven years, since graduating from my MFA in Creative Nonfiction in 2014. I started the memoir as my MFA thesis, though instead of focusing on my own life at the time, I dove headfirst into my maternal grandparents' youthful trans-Siberian journey to Sakhalin Island, where they were sent on work assignment as newlyweds by the Soviet state in the mid-1950s. I suppose I started there because of a desire to "begin at the beginning," which for me was the origin story of my family as I knew it for most of my childhood—the story of Mama, Baba and Deda.

I figured during my MFA that I would eventually get to my own life story after exploring Baba, Deda and Mama's, because mine didn't seem to invite or even allow a head-on approach. Frustratingly, I could not explain my life coherently, even to myself. Memories of my childhood, adolescence and young adulthood seemed to have been atomized and recombined in alien ways, as though having journeyed through and emerged on the other side of a black hole, as though they belonged to someone else.

I was always trying to write about the black hole, but its gravity swallowed all of my words and imagination, so I couldn't seem to make sense of it all. Whenever I tried, I would end up getting sucked back inside it, lured by the need to name what was happening to me in something other than metaphor. I realized I could not write from inside it, but I also couldn't find a lasting way out. I did not even understand what it was in any other terms—only the metaphor could capture the experience in language.

When the black hole swallowed my relationship with Mom and my entire US-based extended family three years into my post-MFA writing drought, I was left to make sense of a story that seemed to have come to its natural conclusion. I thought—well, now I can write it—I no longer have to worry about how my writing will impact those relationships and can just focus on myself. But I couldn't. My throat clenched tighter than ever and writing wouldn't come—only tears, rage, and grief. The special fountain pen that Baba, who had since passed away, had gifted me a decade earlier as a college graduation present had disappeared, and along with it so did strength and hope for writing my story.

Urgent health matters had also been keeping my attention away from writing as I grappled with a new diagnosis of rheumatoid arthritis in my early 30s against the backdrop of ongoing financial stress and the voluntary but excruciating loss of my family. Years went by in a kind of holding pattern, as I struggled to stay employed while managing chronic pain with copious NSAIDs, worrying how I would make it through each subway ride with its jerky train movements pulling on my joints and unruly crowds squeezing me into shapes my body couldn't hold. There was no room in my life for anything other than surviving.

2020 brought everything to a head. In February, I started a new anxiety medication for the first time in 16 years after my old standby had seriously declined in efficacy. Unfortunately, the new drug was a bad match for my chemistry and I descended into the worst condition since my teens, when I thought the black hole was immigration and blamed all of my pain and confusion on the tug of war between two cultures, each of which wanted to claim me in my entirety. March brought Covid to NYC, sending everyone into lockdown. Classes transitioned to online delivery, and I along with the entire faculty of my university were retrained for this format. Though the change was drastic and difficult, because of my declining condition on the new meds, I was privately grateful not to have to leave the house.

This return to the netherworld for the three months I spent on the wrong treatment and then weaning myself off of it prompted an inner reckoning. I saw clearly that no one was coming to rescue me, as in my teen fantasies and visions the first time I descended. Back then, I imagined as I wandered in secondhand evening wear the ornate, pristine halls and gardens of wealthy DC homes and embassies where my pianist mother accompanied at concerts and I turned the pages for her, that someone might see me—see the sadness and hurt in my eyes that my mother could not. The gaze of a handsome man, like in all the fairy tales, would come to rest on me, a long-suffering Cinderella, righting somehow the wrongs of my life, siphoning that sadness like poison out of my mouth with his lips.

Now in my 30s, and already paired to a wonderful, caring partner in spite of my worst fear of being too broken for a healthy relationship, I understood that being loved and seen was not a vaccine against suffering. The damage, such as it was, had already been done, and no amount of fierce loving would ensure that I never felt so horrid again.

It was up to me—a matter of life and death—to find a way out of this place, to find the resources that would make it possible, to trust the love and support that were there for me from my partner, his family and my friends. Ironically, if Covid had not created the space and time for me to rest, reflect, and research, I would never have been able to get to this important insight. I needed the interruption to my routine of barely hanging on — a break from constantly pushing myself to squeeze out the last dregs of my energy to keep my job — so that I could glimpse the sadness and hurt in my own eyes and refuse to look away.

Little by little I started to dig my way back to myself. I changed medications, restarted therapy and seeing my rheumatologist again after a years-long financially imposed pause. I returned to meditation after a decade-long hiatus and began spending more time walking the park across the street from home as the warmth of spring beckoned and the stay home order was lifted. The black veil too began to lift, just a little, but I knew there was so much more work to be done, that I would have to commit to caring for myself differently this time, like it was my job, my most important job. Like I wished that Mom could have decades ago.

Building on this progress, I started reading more online about what might connect all of my issues together. Over the course of my research, I came to understand more and more deeply that what I had been looking for had been right in front of me all this time. The black hole had a name in the literature of psychology. It was called complex trauma. And my most recent brush with it prompted me to finally walk away from my family, though it started long ago, in the earliest of childhood. Trauma explained the fragmentation, the shame, the memory issues, the confusion, the inflammation and aggression of my immune system which expressed itself as arthritis. It explained my reliance on metaphor—language ceases to exist in trauma states or becomes meaningless, broken down into sounds and rhythms, textures and colors and images, sensations and emotions swimming together in a turbulent primordial soup from which something living has the potential to emerge but which lacks the coherence of life itself.

On some level I had known what the black hole was since my teens, but having been raised to thoroughly mistrust my own experience and perceptions by a family shaped by Soviet oppression and unwilling to examine its dysfunction, I suppressed this knowledge until recently. Now everything I read kept confirming my experience—what I felt made perfect sense when looked at through the lens of complex trauma. The black hole had felt so dangerous because it fed on light and was therefore invisible. Now it was as though I had access to astronomical blueprints that proved its existence by its effect on me—the symptoms it created in my nervous system that otherwise had no coherent explanation.

I applied for sabbatical armed with new knowledge, but still far from certain in my success. Would the writing come now that I had this validation in my instincts? It didn't seem so straightforward, but I knew I was ready to try again.

This was my first ever sabbatical—a privilege I could not believe I had been granted in the way that any good fortune feels suspect to one knocked down once, twice, thrice too many times. I'd saved up money from an extra class I taught in the pandemic fall of 2020 so that I could take not only fall 2021 to write but also the summer preceding it to focus on bolstering my nervous system. As that time approached, I felt the familiar lump in my throat that accompanies a foray into my psyche. Of course, avoiding those forays was equally useless in protecting me from the pain and confusion of separation from the self—just because it was not staring me in the face did not mean I was ever really free of the shame and sense of brokenness I felt particularly sharply when examining my fractures.

As soon as I approached to look at myself more closely, the cacophony of voices in my head demanding that I get with the program and write, dammit, blaming me for failing, pushing, pulling, and stretching me into unnatural shapes and postures, would go dead silent. Like the observer effect, but with my inner world. Just as I readied the lassoes of my intellect, of words, to grasp my inner experiences, as soon as they saw me coming, seemingly before I even took a step toward them, they would transform into clouds of smoke and dissipate, leaving me disoriented and defeated in a void from which I could perceive nothing but the shadows of my shame and failure blocking out all the light of the world.

In my research I found an online class I could take to help address the impact of trauma on my nervous system that caused such great swells and surges of panic and such swooping swings into deadening depression in my body. I wanted to learn how to ride the dangerously powerful waves of feeling and sensation without getting sucked back into the singularity. The course lasted most of the summer and I learned a lot about the functioning of the nervous system and how it can stay stuck in a protective response after an event or series of events that prove too much for the organism to handle.

Like many other course participants, I realized I had been stuck in a protective nervous state for decades and learned that the path to a regulated, healthy system is non-linear, requiring patient self-exploration and the daily practice of deeply multilayered self-care for the rest of my life. I learned breathing, journaling and movement practices that help settle the body and mind and improve communication and energy flow between them. Though incredibly helpful, I could see that my new skills were unlikely to result in the sweeping nervous system healing I needed to help me finish the draft of my memoir by the end of the year. Still, having acquired a beginner's toolkit for my nervous system by the last week of August, I was all set to start my draft on September 1st. Miraculously, that was also the week I discovering while searching for something else altogether Baba's fountain pen lodged in the cushions of the couch where I had looked frantically many times before but never found it.

Writing went smoothly all of September. I got to 20,000 words of my memoir and celebrated a budding almost daily writing practice. But then something shifted and October came and went with only a handful of pages written, pages that bothered and displeased me like naughty children, refusing to listen and follow instructions. I felt lost again, even with my new emotional self-care toolbox, and entirely daunted by my task.

In November, I told myself I would pick back up again after a month of soul searching. I did start writing again, but what came out was this essay—not my memoir. This feels like a kind of failure and a kind of success.

I only realized that the term complex trauma had anything to do with me less than two years ago, and every month I learn something new, something that opens new doors inside of me. This essay was started the day after a 75-minute online Internal Family Systems workshop. IFS is a therapy modality based on the phenomenon of internal fragmentation that develops as a result of complex trauma. According to IFS, the parts of me that need me to write and the parts that are terrified of trusting my own truth to myself and others are in a constant battle. I asked the teacher about the void I faced when I sat down to write—how when I tried to access my parts, the voices inside of me, everything went dead and I felt entirely cut off from myself.

"The void," she said, "Hmm, sounds like a protector part."

"You mean the void is not an absence but a part itself?" I clarified.

"What do you think it's trying to protect you from?"

I considered the question. The one thing the void spared me was the confusion of all of the voices inside talking, yelling, screaming over each other and paralyzing me in self-doubt. By keeping the voices at bay, the void was shielding me from suffering.

"The cacophony," I answered after a moment.

And with that the void became a door and I walked through it.

Audrey Roth

The Light of My Soul

I wish I could tell you all the pain's in your head
That it all would be better if you'd just do what they said
But if the voice that is talking is never your own
Then who's gonna tell you, you've finally come home?

—"Never Your Own," music and lyrics by Ferron

My family was all about home—first, the garden apartment in which we lived until I was five years old, and then our house, where I lived until I was 20. My dad and mom lived there after, one by one, their children flew the coop. My dad lived there until two days before he died—alone, in a hospital bed, where he lay in restraints because he kept trying to get out of bed to go somewhere (he never knew where, sadly). My mom stayed at the house until it became her prison, rendering her unable to leave as a result of frequent falls and stairs no longer manageable. At age 85, having vowed she was "born a New Yorker, lived [her] whole life in New York, and would die in New York," I somehow convinced her to move to Massachusetts to be near me.

There was a lot of history in that home of theirs. Birthdays and anniversaries, New Year's Eve parties, Rosh Hashanah dinners, break-fasts at the close of so many *Yom Kippurim*. But also my dad's brutal towering drunken rages, lashing us as brutally as any cat-o'-nine-tails, leaving welts and permanent scarring on our souls. There was no respite, no repair. The pain went too deep for any hope of healing.

My parents vehemently insisted that this was our home. The five Roths—Eleanor and Phil at the top of the pecking order, my sister and brother below them, and, finally, me at the very bottom. I used to think of it as Hell, not Home.

Our parents forbade us from staying overnight at a friend's house. No sleepovers, no slumber parties; my dad insisted that we could stay out late, but either he or our mom would pick us up to come home. No sleep-away camp for my sister or me (my brother went to a boy scout camp one summer). Who knows what might have happened to us if they had allowed it? My dad clearly understood the danger of other fathers running amok. That guilty pleasure was reserved for him alone.

As I grew up, I never felt like I had a home. The concept of "home," with its attendant safety and love, was anathema to me. I went "back to the house," never "home." You can see why, right? I certainly could.

In my *Shul*, there's a prayer we often sing at services, instead of the traditional, somber *Barechu*:

> *Barechu, dear One*
> *Shechinah, holy name*
> *When I call on the light of my soul*
> *I come home*

For the longest time, this prayer ate at me. Sometimes, I would leave the sanctuary during it. I rarely sang it—it made me feel like I didn't belong. Finally, I talked to my Cantor about it.

What does it even mean, to "come home," Beth? I don't have a home. I've never had a home. I don't know if I even believe there's such a thing. I feel so uncomfortable singing this—it feels almost like a sin, like I'm praying about something I don't understand or believe in.

Beth looked at me with her always-kind eyes, her face exuding genuine empathy. I felt enfolded and understood.

Maybe "home" doesn't have to be a place, Audrey. Maybe it can be inside you, or in your relationship with God. You definitely have a oneness with God.

Yes, I do. But that's different—it's personal, and private, and kind of metaphysical. Know what I mean?

Absolutely, I do. I wonder if you might think of this prayer as aspirational, since it's not your reality.

I could do that. Although I wasn't sure it was something I aspired to.

Sometimes, after that conversation, I would sing with the rest of the community, as we stood together for the *Barechu*. Much of the time, though, I would hold the *Siddur* (the prayer book) close to my heart, close my eyes, and listen. I wasn't sure exactly what for. Understanding? Agreement? God? I just didn't know.

I put "home" on my therapy bucket list, "to boldly go where no [trauma survivor] has gone before." As you might imagine, this list was voluminous, and I was forced to prioritize. While it wasn't relegated to the bottom of the list, it also didn't rise to the top. Flashbacks came first, with work issues, and developing and maintaining a healthy, loving relationship with my Deb rounding out the top three. These, not surprisingly, took up most of my therapy time.

But slowly, stealthily, *Barechu, Dear One* worked its way front and center, becoming a critical element of my healing. Realizing that without embracing "home," my relationship with Deb would be stuck in limbo-land, and I wouldn't be able to experience it (or my love for her) as deeply and completely as I yearned to do.

I needed to de-anathematize the concept of "home." To move it onto my "let's think about it" list from my humongous "feh, I hate this" detritus pile. It took some digging to locate it, let me tell you.

After innumerable therapy sessions and cogitation *ad nauseam*, one day, at the end of a particularly stressful time at work, during which nothing was going right, I was on the verge of a meltdown. I thought, *I want to go home to my Deb.*

Suddenly, I had a home!

Where love and safety lived, instead of the ghosts of the marauders of my childhood.

I was home.

At last.

Barechu, dear One ... when I call on the light of my soul, I come home.

Imogene!

My grownup asked me if I want to write about me today.

I say yes. But I can't write. Cuz I'm only three.

So I tell her what I want to say. She writes it down. I tell her don't fix it so it sounds like you!

Cuz I'm real smart.

And I'm real funny. Wanna hear a joke?

> *What did the spider ask the fly?*
> *I don't know, why?*

Get it? Get it?

My grownup always singed that song. You know, right?

> *There was an old lady who swallowed a fly*
> *I don't know why she swallowed a fly*
> *Perhaps she'll die*

Our mommy singed it to us, and we loved it! We laughed and laughed!

My favorite part is about the spider that wriggled and jiggled and tickled inside her.

My grownup's name is Audrey. You know her. Right?

Me and my grownup used to be the same age. We used to be the same person.

We stopped that when I was three.

Now my grownup is really really really old. I can't even count that big.

Not me. I'm still three.

My name is Imogene.

My grownup used to be with this lady. Robin is her name. Robin gived me that name when she meeted me a long time ago. Like three million gazillion years ago.

Before that I was always Audrey. But Robin knowed I needed my own name.

Imogene! I love that name!

Do you love it too?

I think my grownup didn't like me so much.

I keeped sorta knocking at her brain to say hi to her. But she keeped not answering me.

You want to know why?

Good. Cuz I'm gonna tell you.

A really really bad thing happened when we was three years old.

It was horrible and terrible and really really really really scary.

Our daddy did something so so so bad to us.

We loved our daddy a lot before that.

I remember when we was really little and we would listen to him when he was sleeping.

He snored A LOT!

I liked that. It maked me feel all warm and happy. Cuz he was with us.

He would wake up and smile big at us. He loved us.

We loved him.

I remember the good smell of him when we was little.

We would sit on the couch sometimes. Us and our daddy.

One time he falled asleep on the couch.

We was laying on his chest and his arm was holding us. We goed up and down every time our daddy breathed. It was like a ride!

He snored and we falled asleep too all happy and safe.

59

Then our mommy came into the room and she was mad at our daddy.

You could have smothered her, Phil! (That was our daddy's name.)

Our daddy wouldn't have did that.

He never hurted us.

I have a big sister named Suzie. I love her!

She taked care of us a little. We played. Suzie made us laugh. We giggled a lot.

It feeled like that silly spider that the old lady swallowed!

One time our Daddy did a terrible awful thing to us. He didn't have no underwear on and we seed his big ol' thing coming toward us.

He made us open our mouth real big. Really really big. And he sticked that thing into our mouth.

He kept pushing it and pushing it into our mouth. It got terrible big. It hurted so bad.

And we couldn't breathe. We feeled sick.

Then all this yucky stinky stuff was in our mouth. His thing got smaller and he taked it out.

He told us not to tell our mommy. And he leaved.

I think maybe Suzie seed what our Daddy did, because her bed was right next to ours.

Maybe she wished she could do something. Maybe run and get our mommy.

I think maybe it maked her stop laughing forever. Suzie was scareded all the time after that.

Suzie couldn't help me. Nobody could.

After that time I hated him.

Me and Audrey became different kids.

The other me left me. She growed up. I stayed me. I stayed three.

We didn't talk to each other for a long long time.

But I knowed that sometimes when things happened to her she remembered.

I knowed. Because she hurted a lot sometimes.

My grownup is real smart. I know that. She doesn't know that. So she's stupid too! (Now I'm giggling!)

But see—when she's hurting like that she can't use her words. It's like they're playing hide and seek with her.

(I love to play that game!)

She just curls up like she's a big ol' ball and she keeps saying *ow ow ow ow ow*. It used to take a long time for her to be like my grownup again.

Then my grownup had a baby. She was still with that Robin lady. I felt a little sad because my grownup loved that baby so much.

Now she's never going to love me.

That's what I thinked.

When her baby was three, my grownup started thinking about what our daddy did to us. That's how old we were when our Daddy hurted us so terrible bad.

I wanted her to think about me too. And know that I'm still here.

But she stopped thinking about it. I started crying. I was really scareded I was gonna be alone forever.

Sometimes I don't breathe so good.

And I'm real real lonesome.

I wanted to make us die. So I won't be by myself any more. But it never happened.

It took more and more years until my grownup talked to me.

Her baby was seven. That's how old Suzie was when this thing happened to us, and Suzie stopped laughing.

My grownup started to talk to this really nice lady named Caroline. I liked her a whole lot.

One day my grownup remembered that I am here. When she and Caroline was talking about what our daddy did to us. I was so happy!

Me and my grownup started to talk. She tells me she loves me and she's sorry.

She starts to cry. I start to cry. We kinda hug.

Now we love each other. A lot!

We go this place called Shul. And pray.

My grownup sings these things called prayers.

We talk to God during this Amidah prayer. I get to tell God how I feel and it's ok.

My grownup takes care of me. She hears me when I'm sad. And we cry.

We tell each other jokes. And we laugh.

We even sing about that silly ol' lady who swallowed a fly.

It feels real good.

WILLIAM CONSIDINE

Being Bullied

Ninth grade was a rough year. The school district's change to a junior high system was brand new. Some ninth graders were much bigger than eighth graders, and bullying was rampant. All the kids talked crudely about sex, whatever that was, and it was still a bit unclear.

Things got better in high school. By the start of junior year, I was serving on the school newspaper, active in Speech Club and known for being smart. I was also persuaded by a friend to join the cross-country running team that Fall. That involved frequent 2.5-mile races with other schools through various parks and along roads. I wasn't very good at it. It was painful, but I persisted. I had a team uniform. After school, I changed into uniform in the locker room then ran in front of the school and across the street into the park where we trained.

For the school newspaper, I submitted a signed editorial against the snobbishness of clothes-shaming and the domineering focus on fashions among boys. You had to have a camel-colored, V-neck sweater and the right kind of jacket, a certain brand name, available in off-white or blue. A couple clothing stores downtown were emphasized as the places to find these essential garments, and the store names figured prominently in bragging and taunting.

My editorial was published and created a storm. My first inkling was in gym class, when we boys were in our gym clothes in a straight line along the edge of the basketball court, waiting for the gym instructor to emerge eventually from his office. One fellow stepped out of line to yell at me for the editorial and kick me in the rear, in front of everyone. Then I was mortified to learn that because my editorial had named the stores that were cited in taunting, and they were owned by Jews, that my editorial was being accused by adults of anti-Semitism. At least one complaint was made to the school. (I believe the school newspaper's faculty advisor and the senior editors should have recognized in advance the hazard of naming the stores. And so should I!) I couldn't believe what was happening, the misunderstanding and accusation. They were just stores.

About this same time, in another gym class session, we boys had to climb a rope all the way to the rafters, one at a time in front of each other. I knew what was at stake but couldn't do it, I was afraid of heights. In the whole class, only one other boy and I didn't climb to the top. This marked me as weak, at a bad time.

There was a group of guys from the suburb White Oak (and I recognize now that the name for this relatively new suburb perhaps had a racial gesture in its name, as a haven from the multiracial industrial city's urban core) who started picking on me. It was attitudes like theirs that I had criticized in the editorial. I was chiding their jokes and taunts about other people's clothing. They were a richer group and full of themselves. Some had cars. They were not Jewish.

At this time, a girl from White Oak spoke to me in the cafeteria at lunch, saying that she was friends with the popular evening DJ on the local rock-and-roll radio station, and he wanted to invite me to appear on his radio program to discuss my editorial. I declined, out of mortification at what the editorial had already cost me. (Of course, I should have accepted!)

Several of this clique heard this offer. They were in my geometry class. They also apparently resented how readily I caught on to geometry. They took my geometry textbook in the cafeteria and passed it around, smashing food on multiple pages, which stuck the pages together, making it largely unreadable and useless. They warned me not to tell on them. This clique started calling me "Whitey" after a boy who had recently supposedly run away with the circus when it had been in town. They accused me of masturbating (!) like him. Being a masturbator was a key element in being like Whitey. (I think poor Whitey, whom I had only heard of, had been bullied terribly, and maybe joining the circus was just a cover story for his actual whereabouts with relatives or otherwise.) My work in geometry plummeted at once. The teacher soon noticed that I had no textbook, so he gave me another.

In chemistry class, one of this clique sat behind me and another sat beside me. When the teacher was out of the room, the one behind me (let's call him George) started jabbing me in the back with a pencil. The tip suddenly broke off in my back. I worried that this alien thing was in my back and might have further consequences like blood poisoning. (I still have the small scar.) I left class to go to the student nurse. My parents were called and came to the school, my dad in his plumbing clothes. George was easily identified, from sitting behind me, as the one who had jabbed me in the back, but I don't know that he suffered any consequences for his mere adolescent mischief.

After that, his friend sitting beside me (let's call him Jack) started taunting me that I had "told on" George. Couldn't I stand up for myself instead of running to the school nurse? Was I afraid to fight? No? Would I fight with Frank (a boy I'd never met, whom the clique apparently admired for having had boxing lessons and driving a sporty car)? No, I had no quarrel with Frank. What about Jack himself? Did I think I could beat up him? I said, "I don't know if I could beat you up, but I'm not afraid of you." Well, Jack said, why don't we see? Let's see if you're afraid to fight me.

I could see clearly that I was targeted for more bullying, with many incidents already (the kicking, the geometry book destroyed, the pencil stab in the back, and their derision of me as the new "Whitey"). So, I had to fight. It was quickly arranged for after school in the park. I got a friend to serve as my second. After school, I went to the designated place in the park, and soon the clique came in their cars. Some friends of mine came too. I think there were about eight onlookers.

I wasn't afraid of a fight, but I was afraid of getting caught and getting suspended from school, a black mark that would, I feared, ruin my hopes for a college scholarship. Even so, I had to fight to show that there were consequences for pushing me around.

And so, I had a fist fight after school in the park, in the fall of eleventh grade, sixteen years old. We punched each other several times in the face, then grappled. As he was somewhat bigger than me, he ended up on top, knelt on my arms and slapped my face several times. He asked me to say, "Uncle" and slapped me again and again. I thought of getting out from under him, by bringing my feet up under his armpits and using my leg strength to topple him. I feared that then the fight could grow in intensity, with more extensive injuries, and a school suspension would loom. I said "Uncle" and it was over. We shook hands. I took pleasure in pointing out the bruised lip I'd given him.

And the bullying stopped!

My brother Jim heard about the fight at school and told my Dad, and Dad was solicitous. He wanted to know how I felt at the time. I told him I thought it was so stupid, that these kids from White Oak were jealous of me because I was on an athletic team (the cross-country running team) and they weren't, and I was much better in school too, so they picked on me and I had to fight one of them. He asked how I felt at the time, and I said that the main thing I felt was how BORING it was, to have to go through all this nonsense for these assholes.

I had read about young Abe Lincoln fighting a group of bullies, one at a time, and he beat each of them. I felt badly that I didn't engage further, didn't topple him off me, didn't win. But net, I realized Lincoln didn't face a potentially ruinous suspension from school, and I had done what I had to do, navigated a tough situation successfully. I'd shown, by adolescent standards, that I was potentially a man.

As for the other matter, the apparent adult allegation of anti-Semitism, I soon made two new friends in high school through Speech Club, both Jewish, who became my best friends. And in Speech Club and AP English was the beautiful, talented, warm Jewish girl who also became a good friend and would become my wife.

Nina Glueckselig

Confessions of a Hoarder of Beauty

I live in a five-bedroom house that is filled with the possessions of a life well lived. But will this be a burden to my children? I am afraid for them to find out the number of possessions I have, to the point of shame. So much money tied up in everything I have, borne out of the lust for beautiful things. Is this my legacy and will it mean something to them? Or will they say, "What was she thinking?"

My father's family were antique dealers. My father grew up in an artistic and creative environment. They had to give everything they had in their apartment to the Gestapo as a tax to gain the papers they needed to escape Austria. My father and uncle came to New York with eight dollars between them. Hearing a story like that repeatedly during my childhood fueled my desire to replace what they lost and more. I had to do better.

Let's start with the obvious: There's a room full of beads of every kind you can imagine: semiprecious and precious stones of garnet, peridot, lapis, iolite, sugilite, kyanite, amber, pearls, ruby, sapphire, emerald, hand-blown glass beads from Venice sometimes with spots of gold metallic reminiscent of Klimt. Little orbs of color and light. Tray upon tray of handmade sterling beads from Indonesia, India, and Thailand. A kilo of silver is worth $900. I might have 25 kilos. That's the thing, I don't know. When I was designing jewelry my desire for beads was insatiable. Whatever money I made in large part went back into buying more beads. I went to trade shows and showrooms. Buying hanks of beads that I had to touch, to communicate with. I couldn't wait to get back to my studio and start combining elements of every color, size and shape.

There are spools of leather, silk, chain, waxed linen in every color, bags of tassels. There are the finished pieces of jewelry, multi-stranded necklaces of gemstones and silver, incorporating leather, chain, African trade beads, silver, wood. I designed pearl necklaces for bridal parties and custom-made necklaces with beads of every size and material. No two pieces are the same.

On every surface in the house one might find a piece of jewelry or a bead. Change purses with rings, pins, a piece of leather with a dangling charm, a marble, one earring from a pair bought in Israel at age 16 and other mismatched earrings. How does an earring follow you from place to place your whole life?

I own fine jewelry—gold chains, pendants, turquoise rings and earrings, gold and silver hoops, a pair of rose gold and emerald earrings called "The Wave", purchased at Aaron Faber, a fancy gallery in New York City between Fifth and Sixth Avenues. A $1,000 instant sale, just exercising my credit card with no doubt in my mind. I begged my future husband for the $10,000 Tiffany ring with vine curlicues in platinum and diamonds as my engagement ring. I inherited my family's jewelry, the pieces that somehow survived the war—gold watches, a delicate Victorian necklace with a diamond and emerald pendant, charm bracelets, art deco pins. I turned a garish diamond ring into a rectangular pendant with a diamond on each corner.

I can always see my mother dressed in dresses she sewed herself with matching shoes and purses. Everything had to match. I'm the opposite. The more chaotic my style the better. She lost everything too and rebuilt a collection of clothes and jewelry.

So that's true confessions about jewelry. Let's move on to bags.

First there's my Prada ruffle bag for $2,000, a Prada crossbody for $700. Two Fendi spy bags with braided handles in mahogany and beige —$2,000 each. I'm trying to sell them on Poshmark, but secretly I want to keep them. Five Sak bags crocheted of recycled fabric that have a feel of raffia, worth about $800. I even picked out colors to customize a couple of them which they handmade for me in Indonesia.

Quietly letting the customer peruse the lovely bags in a shop on a small canal in Venice, Señor Balducci, the owner, let the irresistible handmade bags speak for themselves. I even ordered one from across the ocean, wiring the money over and impatiently waiting for DHL delivery.

I worked for a year at a high-end leather store in Cleveland called Fount where a 50 percent discount led me to acquire a beautiful collection of bags, a cross body belt bag shaped like a fanny pack, a backpack, the Bellfield tote in two sizes, the Grand and the Classic, the Kinsley cross body, the Coventry backpack. Bags handmade in Cleveland and Mexico. Durable, elegant, functional.

Then there is Anushka: hand painted bags—cactus theme, floral garden, medieval village, air balloons over the countryside. Bags that started off as a canvas of white leather meticulously hand painted in India.

There's more: Vera Bradley bright floral quilted bags and small purses, random silk and crocheted bags, bags of woven leather. But you get the idea.

Now we can move on to pens.

The most obvious is $600 spent on a pretentious Visconti Homo Sapiens fountain pen that doesn't even fill up easily. An attending physician in the hospital had it clipped to his pocket on his lab coat, so I had to have one. It is so sophisticated, I thought. But it's ridiculous, a rip-off because it runs out of ink within a few pages of writing. There are even YouTube videos trying to explain how to fill it. For that money, there should be a plunger and chamber you can see filling up. Without going into too much detail it does not. It's too fabulous to even fill up like a normal fountain pen.

I went through a Lamy fountain pen kick where I bought fifteen pens with different colored barrels, filling them up with matching colored Iroshizuku inks from Japan. Ina-ho a brownish gold, Yu-yaki, red, Murasaki-shikibu, purple. I got bored with this and the pens all dried out. At home waiting for surgery, I thought it would be a fun project to fill them up again with different colored inks and use them to draw with. I have a special leather clutch from Fount that I carry them in.

I own a Montblanc pen, a sterling pen from Tiffany's, and a fountain pen with musical notes engraved on the barrel. Then there are all the inks I use to fill them up, and refills for my less expensive roller ball pens. It all started with my father drawing with one Rapidograph pen and a fountain pen for writing. He did not need all the things I did, but I feel safe with them around me.

Take a look in my closet and there's a whole world of fashion going on in there. There's no type of clothing I don't like. Wool and silk scarves, all kinds of leather shoes, cowboy boots, clunky ankle high boots and sandals, crocheted sneakers. I love heavy hand knitted sweaters from Ireland.

I am very partial to Eileen Fisher, a New York based designer who started her multimillion-dollar international business in 1984 with five samples on a rack at a trade show. She has simple, elegant clothes made of fine fabrics, silk, cotton and linen. I finally said goodbye to the first pair of pants I ever bought from her 30 years ago in aquamarine with subtle black stripes.

There's a designer on QVC that I love also that is totally different than Eileen. Her name is Lori Goldstein, and her clothing line is called LOGO. She's a former stylist for the stars, having worked with the likes of Annie Leibovitz. Her pieces are feminine with flounces and lace, with bright painterly patterns; she and her co-conspirator Amy Stran wear you down with their enthusiastic description of every single piece they are selling. I tape the show and fast forward through the repetitive parts, but all too often I see something, and I say to myself, "Hmmm, that's kind of cute." I imagine myself twirling around in their tank dress with the six-inch broomstick hem with my hands in the pockets (everything must have pockets and tight armholes). The next thing I know I am on my phone clicking away to purchase my newest dress which will come home with me on four easy payments. Everything goes with everything she says, and I believe it. A good day is wearing Lori and Eileen together.

So, I've arranged my closet in a LOGO section, Eileen Fisher, Amazon basics—crew neck pullovers and sweats and then other random designers. The Gap, Soft Surroundings, J. Jill. When I try to give things away to a friend, they ask me if I really want to. Yes, please, let's make some room in the closet.

Finally, there's are the art materials. My preferred medium is pastels and I have a collection of many sets like Prismacolor, Cretacolor, Derwent, Jack Richeson, Grumbacher, Caran D'ache, Conte a Paris, Holbein, Schminke. Every set has tonal variations of colors and a different feel when applied to the paper. I have watercolor pencils and pencils for coloring and drawing. Many distinct types of paper from canvas to pastel to watercolor or multimedia. I'm whimsical in how I choose what set to work with and my art is spread around the house from the sunroom to an upstairs studio and most recently the dining room table. I love metallics and layered pastels with acrylic markers and paint. I say I am influenced by Paul Klee, Gustav Klimt and Wassily Kandinsky, but think this is grandiose on my part. My father was the artist, not me.

My house is built out of all these elements, not plaster or wood. My house is held up by shelves of paints and markers, paper, gemstone treasures. Things with texture, shape, quirky and edgy. I am a hoarder of beauty.

Julius the Dog

I never had a dog before. I always had the fantasy of having a puppy, jumping on me, licking me, thrilled to see me even after a moment's absence. My parents said, "Will you walk the dog?" Case closed.

I don't know how to write about something positive.

I'm committed to anxious afraid sad scared.

I see him on Facebook and pick him out of a video of four puppies chasing each other. He is white with a large black spot on his back. I say to my husband,

This is my dog.

I am recovering from a suicide attempt.

Some friends think a dog is a bad idea.

You're too vulnerable, they say.

What about the cats?

Do you actually think you will walk him in the winter?

He will get very big.

"How long do Bernedoodles live?" my son Max asks me.

"If he lives 12 years you will be 77."

"That's too old to have a dog."

He is calculating my demise.

Why do others think they know what is best for me?

What about the advice I always get not to project myself too much into the future?

The eager euphoric endearing movement of his tail thumping against the wood floor

I know

This is my dog.

I'm connected to him,
    I know this for certain; no one can tell me otherwise.

This is my dog.

My therapist laughs at what people have been saying to me,
and tells me he likes the idea.
    Ellie says this might just be "the ticket".

I raised my children
    they put everything in their mouths and
    I had to watch their every move.
    They were eager euphoric endearing puppies
    I took care of them; I bathed them,
    toweled their hair dry and held them close
    when they cried.
    They drilled their heads into my shoulder
    and I told them everything would be okay,
    even if I knew it couldn't possibly always be okay;
    I was convincing myself also.

We meet Julius Q. Pupster,
    a name my husband Bill came up with and it feels right.
    I watch him trot from person to person in the breeder
Denise's living room.
    He jumps on me and licks my face.
    He doesn't know if the small world he inhabits will be kind
to him.

How can someone hurt an animal?
How can someone hurt a child?
I have a chance to make the life of a living being better.
I want that.
This is who I am, a mother,
A mother to my parents,
my children,
my patients.

I love him already and that is because
This is my dog, don't you get it?

In the mornings before he comes, I lie in bed. What was the point of getting up? My whole life I had a purpose. I would get up even if I didn't feel like it.

I'd shower and dress and get my children up. I was always hurrying, to work, the grocery store, driving my children to school and music lessons.

Making dinner.

Lather, rinse, repeat.

Tedious, but full of joyful laughter, intense tears.

Now I write a gratitude list. I write my morning pages. I try to put the images of downing all the pills out of the movie screen of my mind. I am still convinced I have had a good life and it was a good time to make an exit. But I survive and I am not at all glad about it. I am tired of the hospital where time passes so slowly and the food tastes like moldy sponge. People talk in the halls during the night and I cannot sleep. The hospital is no place to get better. I go home and face what I did.

I thrash my legs around and turn from side to side.

But I think of the dog every morning in the dark of my room. I feel hope. I look at the videos Denise texts me of him. Joy. So pure and precious. Running towards life. I see him running towards me, hearing his feet thump on the ground, and the dark lightens. I want to be there in the morning when he gallops toward me, wagging his tail. I make myself get up.

My father was always glad to see me.

I always came home from far away and couldn't wait for him to open the door.

I was glad to see him, too.

I know this will be the same with Julius, because:

This is my dog.

Denise is sick, probably with Covid, so we meet her son-in-law at a McDonald's off of I-90. Like a hostage exchange, I hand him the money in 100-dollar bills; he hands me the leash and the dog is now mine. We pick up all 21 pounds of him and put him in the back seat of the car. He wriggles beside me, settles down and puts his head on my leg. I tell him he is a good boy and everything is okay. I am telling myself everything is okay.

Okay. Okay. Over and over, okay, and I believe it.

Things weren't okay and now they are.

I run my hand over his curly hair and he lifts up his head and licks me. Okay.

This is my dog.

lisa roma

Starting with the Weather and the Ocean Doesn't Care

The weather doesn't care what neighborhood you live in, or what country you're from, how much money you make or don't, what kind of politics you follow or not, or whether you've lost a loved one, experienced trauma, or lived a magical life, what kind of genius or creative you are, how many regrets you carry within your soul, if you or someone you love has mental illness, or a Nobel prize.

The Ocean doesn't care if you've done your homework, how many books you've read, what kind of artwork you paint, poetry you write, or what time of day or night you visit her sandy shores, in whatever season you choose to come, and as many times during the year you may come. She won't make you feel guilty about not visiting. The Ocean will just say, with her salt-in-the-air-spraying-waves splashing into long reaching ripples spreading into rainbow bubbles of foam that tickle your toes with a chill, or moisten your shoes as you walk near her, watching seagulls standing in the shallow water awaiting tiny morsels or crustaceans to crack open, Welcome.

The Ocean loves you just the same. The Ocean loves when you call her name, Mother Ocean. She hears you, and how you come to her with singing prayers of gratitude and wonder, innocence and sensuality, baring your soul and wanting to enter her with your translucent skin, glowing like a newborn re-entering the saline water of the womb. This is Mother Ocean, teaching you how to be a Goddess, a sparkling mermaid in water, and a priestess on land. You embody the stars, you embody the galaxies, you are a reflection of each other, the moon's throbbing silver orb lifts you with gossamer palms, saying, This is what you need, this is what you have.

The Ocean calls to you with an ethereal soul that caresses the Earth with mothering tides and nourishing minerals, feeding and habituating sperm whales, belugas, orcas and dolphins, sharks, marlins, octopods and eels, starfish and moonbeams, seaweed and coral reefs, clothed like underwater galaxies, where the brave adventurers swim and dive in crystalline waters, blue as aquamarine skies, sharing the wisdom of their aquatic teachers, pulling plastic debris from the throat of a grateful sperm whale, freeing a mother seal from the nylon fishing netting that cut skin while wrapped around her pregnant body, as ancient eyes watch with trepidatious expectation.

This is Earth Day, not a birthday, or celebration, it's just a pardon for a wake-up call to stop polluting.

The Universe loves you,
    I am told.   Like a gold shiny button.

Between Heaven and Earth

I love to watch homing pigeons spin black and silver circles above my head out in the glittering blue, a trail of fluttering for all eyes who see,

in these sunny cold days before spring—

and the tall red maple across the way reaching its slender tendrilled arms with wine-red fingertip buds stretching skyward, tasting cool air,

thirsting for rain with its' roots, with an ever-knowing never-ending patience that winter will eventually end,

painting shadows on the white brick house between us—

as they disappear on a mountainous rooftop beneath the heavens.

I love that poetry is my meditation, a power, accessible AT ANY MOMENT—

And that I am Nature, and Nature is me—

As my arms emulate Tree branches, reaching outward and upward—and

Trees are People, too—Life-givers—responsible for the very oxygen we breathe.

The fresh cut grass of spring smells like cucumbers peeled in summer,

And I can taste the pure water of snowflakes as they land on my tongue during winter.

And the sudden burst of vibrating chartreuse buds on tree heads illuminating the evening air, each spring, infinitesimal worlds within a world, emitting a throbbing pulsation of lights, like those that sparkle during Christmas.

And the weaving colors of autumn's crisp orange and
brown leaves,
    between the end of summer and beginning of winter,
    that flutter and are blown off by the wind,
    Crumbling to the ground, to become one with the mulch,
    that rich smelling soil at the feet of trees, Mother Earth's
seed beds,
    for new growth, and the place where all things must
eventually rest.
    These trees, our intermediaries between Earth and Heaven,
    Are the repositories of birds' nests, where baby bird eggs
hatch, becoming
    The small, feathered things that chirp and grow into
    the dynamic joyful fluttering that mesmerizes.

IRIS GERSH

Untangling My Father

My father, Nat Gersh, was rarely happy. He shared the story how he lived in snowy Connecticut on a farm as a youngster with his parents who had emigrated from eastern Europe, possibly Belarus, Lithuania, Poland or Russia. It was a hard life, one I imagine he would think about in his private thoughts. He talked about it only if we kids complained. Then he would tell us that he had to walk eight miles to school. We had a school bus to pick us up.

Our house in Kerhonkson was on Route 209, a two-lane state road, heavily-trafficked in the summer when tourists came by busloads to the Shawangunks known then as the "Borscht Belt." Those summer months, for a few years' duration, my parents ran a restaurant from our closed-in front porch. Three gas pumps dominated the front yard. My dad pumped the gas. My mother made chicken salad sandwiches and whipped out chocolate malt shakes, endless amounts frothing in a shiny two-quart Hamilton Beach blender. She usually sat with her customers, who were more often neighbors than strangers.

Outside the porch around the corner from the red and yellow tin billboards of LSMFT ("Lucky Strike Means Fine Tobacco"), Beechnut Gum, and Dr. Pepper, my sister Louise and brother Bill rattled around in his homemade jalopy, a four-wheel contraption with impressionist drawings glued onto the sides until the day Louise cleaved her chin on an open nail. My father's reaction: he drove her to the hospital, then hurled the car across the road.

Route 209 over the years became the receptacle for burnt-out toasters, radios, and anything else my father tossed across the road. When my mother travelled to work, he made us dinner. If he burned the hamburgers, he would swear stuff about my mother, and there went the toaster. At the time, I never figured out why he was even home, only later figuring out that he probably had been laid off work and found it humiliating to be home while my mother worked.

While everyone pumped, shook, and rattled, I stayed in the restaurant, playing Mommy's helper. She would send me inside the house to the kitchen to get more malt powder, butter or coffee. Then, mid-afternoon, we rested. My brother, in his early teens, met his friends down the hill in the shed. Louise would groan about after lunch clean-up, and I sat at a desk my father had made for me, solid oak with a tilted top for drawing.

One of these warm summer afternoons when everyone finished chores, I sat at my desk, the sun shining on me and my coloring book. I could hear the wash cycle end in furious spinning. I colored in Betty's hair the obligatory yellow and Veronica's black, and then suddenly Archie turned pink and Jughead turned blue. I saw black spots, dropped the crayons, and passed out. My sister shook me awake, a little too hard I thought. Then my father and brother carried me from the porch. I looked up at my brother who said I might be faking it, so I closed my eyes tighter than ever. My mother lay me down gently in my parents' large bed. She applied cold washcloths to my neck, dabbed Vicks on my nostrils, one of her cure-alls for any ailment, and murmured soothing words until I drifted off to a natural sleep with thoughts of my father and brother watching over me.

Some years after I was born, neé Iris Gail Gershowitz, my parents decided to change our last name. There were two families named Horowitz and Markowitz, but my father believed that we needed a less Jewish name. We lived in a predominantly Christian area and though come holidays, the resorts filled with Jewish families mostly from the city, our communities and schools had a small Jewish population. My mother later told me that he wanted to change it to "Gary". She stood her ground, a hard task at times, and said "Gersh" would be fine.

When my friends visited, they heard my father's words, seeming to swell up from way inside him. Some words were in Yiddish like "they" could all "gai in drerd." (go to hell) He could be talking about anyone. Many friends later would tell me that my father was a "rageaholic." A dear friend felt that this was the biggest thing we had in common, angry fathers .One memorable time, he yelled hard and long at my sister and chased her around the house because she had the nerve to walk with a neighbor, Carlos Santiago, through the cornfield. I swung on the hammock feeling glad it was not me being chased. I felt hopeless and powerless as I looked out towards a neighbor's field. My mother yelled at him to stop. Louise confided one evening to her husband and me how the incident affected her. He was abusive, and it traumatized her.

I inherited his love for the country, always in my heart. I knew my father felt sad when he and my mother moved from Kerhonkson, New York, "the country" as all our relatives said, to a larger town, Kingston, not even an hour away. He loved his land, house, chicken coop, and assorted shacks. He and my mother lived in apartments till they finally found the right one. He always worried about her skidding on highways to and from work. When I got older, I realized that he resented her a little. As a high school graduate, she was smarter than he was with "only" an eighth-grade education. His life as a plumber and steamfitter exhausted him. He wanted us to go to college and never have to work as hard as he did. I remember chilly evenings at home when he wrote letters to my brother and sister who were away at college. Every so often I heard him ask my mother, "so how do you spell that, Lil?"

His anger, his very worst behavior, stopped, as many things did, when my mom yelled at him to stop. He tried to diminish her and called her a "dumb ox." Still she was always the peacemaker. I was the youngest in the family, my sister three years older, and my brother a whopping eight years older. I did feel loved by my parents though my siblings thought I was spoiled. During the three years I lived alone with them, I was privy to conversations about my brother being a hippie, and my sister's choices also. In high school I'd get into debates with him, and he told me that I was really smart and that I should become a lawyer. I think that as a teenager, I began to understand more of the family dynamics. Yes to continuing our education, but no to whatever we decided to do in life.

My dad, a union plumber most of his life, told us that politics was all "graft." He detested hypocrisy. At an early age, he shared how people who went to church or synagogue religiously were often the worst hypocrites in their actions. He explained why, but I wish I heard more about those people he admired. I remember him saying, "You can't trust that man as far as you can throw a piano." Only when I got older, I realized that I had a cynical nature which could turn into judgments if I were not mindful. By the time I went to school in Boston, I found plenty to mull over. My first depression was during sophomore year in school.

In my teens and twenties, up until my father died at age 66, I remember only a few occasions seeing my brother and father together. Before he left for Berkeley, my brother had a "happening" at our house in Kerhonkson. My father was kind of excited. He for once was okay with the blasting music, but absolutely no one messing around. He directed traffic to the front yard, and onto the road.

After graduating from a local state College, my brother moved to Berkeley, then northern New Mexico where he helped establish the commune movement. When he did see my father, I remember their hard-headed attitudes toward each other. Most often they argued about values and their lifestyles, neither one giving in. My father hollered about the "damn hippies" calling Bill's friends "dope heads," then blamed my mother for the way her children were turning out. He usually threw in a few bad words about my sister and me. Still, no one got it as bad as my brother.

It finally became my turn to be the "bad" one when I went to college. As they moved me into college the first day, there were all these guys hanging out on the windowsills across from the dorm. My dad said something like, well, you better not be doing anything like that. Those were the years that he wrote me letters. I think they were gold, a mix of his and my mom's daily lives, then pages of rants. My involvement with social activists and belief in activism during those years aggravated him. "I didn't send you to some Ivy League college so you can join the hippies like your brother." At this point, I let go of him emotionally. I knew at heart, like we say in my family, "at heart," he was a good man. He formed us. My father hurt us never with weapons, but with threats. We bore the brunt of his words. There was just so much he was willing to learn and maybe change. He was disappointed in all of us now.

Sometimes he could display a diplomatic side. My college friend Dorine was visiting us in Kerhonkson, New York, and a conversation started about integration, mostly in personal relationships. I went upstairs because my parents did not know that I was involved with a black man. I knew that Dorine could hold her own. She became a labor organizer and already had skills of negotiation and listening intently. I was more fiery and might have exploded. I had the door ajar, and all seemed to be copascetic. Then my father said, "Well, it's going to turn out good, or it's going to turn out bad." My mother laughed a bit and not meanly. Dorine concurred. That one expression became lodged in my brain so that I could allow the world and personal situations to unfold as they would, needing to take care not to internalize so much.

The last time I saw my father was when he and my mother took their first airplane flight and flew to New Mexico. He only agreed to go when she threatened to go by herself. I never saw him as happy when I saw him then, sawing wood, breathing in mountain air, holding his little granddaughters in his lap on the purple leather chair. He confided that the life we were living was pretty much what he had imagined for himself in his older age. He seemed unfazed that my brother Bill and his partner Annie weren't "married". He asked questions of everyone he met and showed interest in all we did. I appreciated his open mind, his almost adjusted attitude towards life. We celebrated my birthday together.

I could tell he was not that happy about my choice, a single woman living a hippie lifestyle. Before they left, my father said that he understood why my brother lived on the mountain, but what the hell was I doing? Why'd I go to college anyway if I ended up living like I did? Who would I meet up here anyway? Yes, I admitted I was loving it all so much, I hardly even cared about going into town (where I might meet someone at a boogie). Then he told me that I could have gone to secretarial school. I had never heard that expectation before, plans for women of the preceding generations. He had repeated over the years that he "busted his ass" to put me through college.

After his visit, my father was back in New York, continuing working with silver, employed as a part-time handyman at a nursing home. A month later, my brother and I flew to New York for my dad's funeral. We were happy that he had gotten to see his granddaughters and that he and Bill had reunited. After he died, I had the feeling that I would never have to meet his standards or feel less than because of my choices. I felt some guilt for the relief I felt. I had always felt his presence when I was in any kind of relationship with a man, how also I would never be able to share or have debates with him.

When I was forty, I had a spiritual coming home to New Mexico. I went to a journal writing retreat in San Cristobal just up the road from D. H. Lawrence's cemetery. All my walks in beauty, the closeness of the participants, my having quit smoking, my staying in my old home, my being gifted with *The Heroine's Journey*, a book about women's odysseys, all of this made me ready for a dream that would re-see our conflicted relationship, one where I always ended up feeling like a loser.

My father and I reunited in our front yard in Kerhonkson, a vision that felt more real than a dream. My dad wore long johns, his skin cool under the morning sun. We are close. I put my arm around his waist. My father spoke simply. "Iris, I love you. There is nothing you ever did wrong. You are wonderful whatever you do, wherever you are." We separated slowly. He has just said all I needed to hear during our lives together. I became lighter and lifted in spirit. After the dream, I renewed faith in myself. I trace his difficulties in life with his own past. Those are my ancestors' stories.

DENNIS FORMENTO

It was insane, but ... just another night

"It was insane, but ...

I sat on the edge of a glacial crevasse and wanted to touch the ice.

"It was insane, but ...

I crossed the border out of East Berlin without a Deutschmark in my pocket, slipping over a turnstile to board the U-Bahn for the West.

I opened my big mouth & started to talk while State Police entered the Capitol building in Baton Rouge & someone thought I was the faculty member who was the leader of the students' demonstration. And then pointed to me when the troopers asked for the leader.

I didn't know there had been a confrontation ornamented with a shouting match at the Governor's Mansion, in which a student threatened the mansion guard with an "insurrection."

I didn't turn around to notice it was a six-foot seven-inch trooper who seized me by the shoulder and spun me around.

These are actually funny at this distance. They were not funny then.

"It was insane, but ...

I remained calm while the airplane shook its way back to New Orleans from Atlanta during an electrical storm. Thankfully I was sitting in the rear of the plane, right in front of a row of Catholic priests.

"It was insane, but ...

Someone thought I would make a good _____.

"It was insane, but ...

I got involved with—her.

"It was insane, but ...

I behaved like a typical man.

I started too many sentences with "I."

"It was insane, but ...

I opened the email.

I clicked the link and a storm of pornographic images poured out of the computer, sex, sex, sex, right in the middle of the writing lab.

I did not need to read about the MC5 during a lull in instructor time.

"It was insane, but ...

I was reading up on the racist right, and had just opened the *Daily Stormer* when a Black student came in and sat next to me.

"It was insane, but ...

It was awfully cold in that prison bunk, Mardi Gras night, and I had promised my girlfriend I would never get arrested again. We had just broken up but I needed her to bail me out of Orleans Parish Prison.

It was a State Trooper once more. They are notoriously incapable of doing proper crowd control, and it was Mardi Gras night, just before 9:30, when the police start clearing the streets. I dropped my bicycle key and bent over to pick it up, when yet another immense trooper ran into my backside and called it assault. "Get inside or go home," he barked just as I reached down for my key. "But Trooper," I said, "It's not 9:30 yet. That's the law." "I'm the law," he said, "and I say get inside or go home."

"But the words on the courthouse say, 'This is a government of law, not of men,'" I said, being a smart ass, and he grabbed me by the shoulders, pulled me backward, and then stumbled over Katia who was squatting in the back door of Café Brasil. The trooper then tumbled over her and slammed into her sister who had just stepped out onto the sidewalk carrying two beers.

"It was insane, but …

Spilling beer on a state trooper can be considered assault on an officer. So the sisters went to jail.

Me, I found myself in the back seat of a NOPD patrol car with the bass player of the Afghan Whigs.

He had just left the studio where the Whigs had been locked up for 96 hours recording a cd.

"It was insane, but …

He had no idea it was Mardi Gras night, and he had just gotten a beer at Café Brasil.

I assured him that his manager would make the bail.

I saw a woman walking calmly with a video camera held low at her knees, casually taping the police riot.

I saw a cop snatch the camera away from her and haul her off too.

And it could have been a lot worse, like the year before, when the cops attacked the Frenchmen Street crowd and dozens of people ran for the R Bar to hide out, but the police already had eighty-five people on their faces in the wet, cold street with its spilled drinks, wee wee and god knows what else.

All that glitter down the drain.

"It was insane, but …

The Afghan Whigs really didn't know it was Mardi Gras.

Stones and Flowers

Flowers flow and stones stand still
to each its own
Stone flowers flow still

The stones—the nightmares and interminable imaginary arguments with people who harass me. "You think you're a genius! You don't want us to understand your poems! Everybody is going to understand MY poetry! You don't want us to—"

The line breaks off. This is a real conflict but not as convincing as the spontaneous reiterations of the nightmares can be.

Four men and a woman sit around a table in a crowded ballroom, there's dense haze—one of the men is speaking, holding everyone enthralled. But he's clearly playing for the attention of the woman, who is young, attractive and hangs on his every word.

The man nudges the guy on his right and points again, subtly, barely raising his finger so as not to be noticed.

But I notice. One can't walk past this person without looking—it's strange what fame will do. I nod involuntarily. It's best, or is it, to keep up a façade of tolerance?

He doesn't look straight at me but smirks and turns his attention back to his bourbon and the young woman next to him, and secondarily to the guys who fill out the table.

"Watch what I am going to do," he says.

Someone at the next table has moved his chair into the aisle. The narrow passage between tables is now narrower and I have to stop, motion to the man, whose attention is not easily gotten, then work my way around him and the five at the next table.

"So," he says.

I nod. That's about all I'm going to give you, I think, but he wants more.

"So, are you still pretending to be a poet?" He smirks. The four companions look on. I look in the other direction.

His smirk turns into a full-blown laugh. He tells me that he hates "fake poets," calls me loser, rich boy, someone who went to MFA school and who believes that poets become poets because "they like to eat."

"Your father is a banker and your mother sits around eating bonbons all day," he says.

That was a cheap shot for such a famed wit, but I keep that to myself. I'm not wealthy. My father was a barber. My mother raised three kids on that income, plus whatever else my dad scraped up taking photographs of babies, trucks, and insurance offices and other barbershops, weddings—whatever he could get to pay off our house in a suburb outside of New Orleans.

The other people at the table all look at me with blank anticipation. What would this poetaster say to the ranking genius of American poetry? Nobody moves. I turn away from the table, the man in the chair in front of me slides his seat almost imperceptibly forward so I can squeeze by. The four at the table with the genius exchange looks and suppress their laughter.

I am able to squeeze by while the famous guy's face brightens into a smile.

"Aw, come on, don't walk away! I am kidding you! Stay, sit with us, have a drink," he says, but of course there is no room for another chair in this standing-room-only house.

"No, thank you," I say.

He leans forward in his chair. "I'll bet you are going to win first prize," he intones, and fishes inside his coat pocket for something—a cigarette? This is a non-smoking venue.

"No, come on," he says, and gestures, the four people at the table, perplexed, start shuffling around, waiting to see what will happen. Should they make room?

The man's face relaxes into a smile. "I'm just kidding you," he says. "Come on, sit with us, let's drink."

The other four seem to want to go along with it, and the woman turns her head to see if there is an empty chair nearby. I turn sideways, my back to the group, to make my way elsewhere.

"You are going to win first prize," he exclaims, and I turn again, to look at him—then decide to turn that look into a stare, a hard, divisive stare, that says, back off. And I know it's a mistake. It is a look that a woman can give and it would be understood in this crowd that she means, "that's enough, leave me alone." It is a sensitive, intelligent, forward-thinking crowd gathered to see some happy contestants win a literary award— but a man, that defensive, to this man? It would be taken as crudely hostile.

I breathe what I think is an inaudible curse.

"Oh, please," he says. As if dismayed. "You see how he is? So aggressive. Go ahead, please leave, we don't want to talk to you."

I lengthen my step, just barely getting my right leg around the man in the aisle.

The famous writer laughs and goes back to his audience— regaling them with a story about his latest journey overseas where a war of liberation had just been fought and he had been invited there to talk about freedom at a writers' conference—a conference much more serious than this festival of accolades and door prizes of which this writer is an acknowledged judge and champion of the writer's life.

Flowers are harder to maintain than stones— because flowers are alive. Flowers flow, stones can only roll.

❧

I'm pretty damned secular but I have a notion of what's sacred. What's old is sacred—what's carbon-dating old is sacred. The trees are sacred, the forests even more sacred, the ancient forests ever more so, the sea—ocean water is deeply sacred and the bones of ancestors are human and sacred. You can study my ancestors' bones. Bring them back when you're done. Knowledge and understanding are sacred uses of bones.

Skin and bones.

Evolution is scientific and miraculous. What are the odds that it could happen again in just this way? The ribs are flat at one end and round at the other, in twelve pairs. The rounded ends attach to joints of the thoracic vertebrae, and the flattened ends reach the sternum in front.

A circle of fifths is perfect, a sequence of perfect fifths: D G D A E B F# C# Ab Eb F. Don't ask. I can't explain but I've heard they're perfect.

What is sacred? The older the better. People treat the Constitution that way even though it was created by a circle of wealthy and privileged white men who did not want to relinquish their wealth and privilege by an act of their own congress. That Constitution was created by humans—and God did not "grant" the laws or freedom, people fought for everything they got, and they are fighting now to read the Constitution as they see fit. They are not always right, but that choice, they believe, is sacred. There are no god-given rights but only rights won by struggle.

God was willing to sit back and watch the struggle—if God was there at all— and sometimes because of the struggle we end up beneath "the beautiful uncut hair of graves." So said Walt Whitman. A little precious, but I know what he means.

✤

What is sacred is good and what is good is the bond between me and my wife. It's not as intense as it once was but that is because we have relaxed into its security, our bond has never been challenged, except by ourselves in our occasional struggles. It's funny but I have no narrative that comes to mind at this time, although there are a lot of stories I could tell.

But I can tell you that I had to wait too long to find her, and so I've never lost the tendency to think, "what if?" What if in my life— what if I had taken another road and moved somewhere else, done something different, married someone other than her. Is she not the flower I wanted, I mean, have I taken a wrong turn? I met Patricia for the second time on a night when a couple of friends, visiting from North Carolina, and I went to the Spotted Cat for swing jazz, and Patricia, leaning against a post, caught my eye. "Are you Dennis Formento?" she asked.

"That depends," I said. "Who are you?"

"I'm Patricia Hart," she said. "You might remember me as Pat Billesbach."

Oh, yeah, I thought, the hair is different, the name is different and it was five years down the road since she had left her husband and moved to Alaska. But I thought—she's someone who can keep a relationship together.

So tonight, remembering that moment seventeen years ago when we met for the second time, I asked her, "When we ran into each other that night at the Spotted Cat, did you think you would like me?"

"No, I just thought, 'Hey, I think that's Dennis Formento. I haven't seen him in a long time.' I hadn't seen her in a long time, too.

Paula Curci

You Know Her

Oh I
I think you know her.
She is the one,
on the day of reckoning,
that will be bargaining
her way out of hell.

Oh I
I think you know her.
She is the one
that calls defeat
and won't complete
any task you give her.

Oh I
know you know her.
She is the one
who wakes you at night,
telling you—you are the one that's hungry—
after she has already eaten the chocolate ice cream.

Oh I
believe you know her.
She is the one
you talk to in your sleep,
the one who whispers in your ear
and looks at you in the morning mirror.

Oh
         you know her.
                          In fact.
     I am
               certain.

Abbondanza!

"Abbondanza!" I yelled
at the head of the table
raising my chianti.
I had full view
of the yard,
of my 'gal' friends.
Surrounding me,
there was plenty
of joy
of support.

"We are lucky girls,"
I reminded them.
We survived.
We are still alive.
"Eat up" I said.
We have plenty,
cold antipasto,
lasagna.

It was one of those days,
you know,
where EVERYTHING was
delicious!
(Pronounce that
DEE- LISH- E- US!)
The air was sweet.
The breeze was cool.

The birds tweeted.
Like in the utopian genre movies,
where everything is alright,
with a perky-happy ending.

Around the table
one by one:
"How did you do it?"
"How was it done?"
They had the tour,
up the spiral staircase
of the carriage house.
I told them, the deed says
'An unmarried woman'!
I laughed.
They chuckled.

"Take a mental picture,"
I spoke.
"We have plenty
of hours,
of moments,
of laughing to do!
But this day,
like all days,
will be over soon.
So, Look around
record what you see.
Not the house.
Not the yard.

Not the furniture.
But you and me.
Let us remember
our worth,
our friendship.
and how it feels to be free …
Abbondanza!"

Dysfunctional Timeline

She was a child
when her name was called
looking through a mirror
a pre-schooler
when she was held down
held
in the hallway
when they began removing her ...

Faking sleep
as a toddler
she ignored her family
so, she could be alone
so, she could run away
from her invader
unable to see
her protector or herself

As a teen
she inhaled
MTV, THC and XYZ
As an adolescent
she was forced
and again
forced
into a submission
of emotional stillness

She was erased
she wasn't blonde
long legged
not enough
not the girl who got the guy
not the thin girl
she was the girl who wasn't …

She was a young adult
when she gorged
late at night
and as an adult
she continued to heave
and heave
gagging on the feelings
she didn't know how to control

At home
she got what she asked for
ignored
the prodigal son
had bigger problems
more important
more severe
louder, meaner

In adulthood
more poor decisions
She never carried
and when she wedded

she married
herself
to gaslights
the kind of love
that doubts

She analyzed
verbal abuse
power misuse
depression
regression
family decay

and how it was ...
swept away
under the rug
for years.

Linda Kleinbub

I Promise Myself

Irregular synapses
penetrated my thoughts
return to yesterday
overgrown
moss

I search the skyline sunset
seeking stars into sight
my steps are guided
evolution entering
life

Living, floating eyes open
clouds hang high
I promise myself
to work on recovery
to try to hold steady

on rocky shores
I promise myself to face fear
for I am told
behind fear
the story gets told

Frigid

We traveled together, an existence of family.
Now we live a routine
filled with chores and "What's for dinner?"

I seek quilted comfort
resist speaking about your bad behavior.
We live like roommates.

I may bear grudge what you have become
I can't change you.
I stay sheltered, closed-mouthed,

write emotions in a notebook,
my life is in revision mode, unsure
how long speechlessness will survive.

Victory at Vacation Day Camp

Vacation Day Camp was a city-run program in New York City in the 1970s. My local public school was transformed into a place where one could play basketball or bumper pool, make arts and crafts or learn a new dance move. It was a safe haven for kids during the sweltering days in the city.

At the end of the summer, a track and field Olympics of public-school programs was held. When I was 11 years old, I was assigned to the long jump. For weeks I practiced standing at a chalk line and jumping with my two feet together. I was an awkward, tall, lanky kid at that age. I practiced every day without much improvement. "Hang in there, kid," my coach encouraged me.

On the day of the event, about 100 kids from all over Queens were spread out on Newtown High School's athletic field. The long-distance and sprinters were hanging around the running track, while the jumpers and javelin throwers were assembled around the edges. There was a lot of standing around as we waited for our event. I got to watch many of the athletes compete before it was my turn. There were different types of jumping events. The biggest mistake one could make was to step on the takeoff marker board, which resulted in instant disqualification, or to fall backward, as the distance jumped was measured from the marker board to the location the closest body part landed. Hence, if someone fell backward the length of their body would subtract from the distance their feet landed. As jumpers were in the air their teammates would often shout, "Lean forward, lean forward!"

To my surprise, the event I participated in wasn't a standing long jump but rather a running long jump. Contestants would run as fast as possible, then leap when they approached the takeoff marker. Maybe my tall lanky body could serve me well. When it was my turn, I ran at my highest possible speed, leaped with all my gusto, remembering to lean forward. I made three good runs and my best score was noted.

To my surprise when the winners were announced my name was called for first place! I went up to the podium and received a small gold trophy. Walking home with my coach later that day he said to me. "You did pretty good today, kid. Who knew you had it in ya? You were so bad during practice I had your name crossed off the list."

ANDREA NICKI

Grandmother's Quilt

I pull my ancestors around me, imagining a warm and cozy great-great grandmother's quilt, but it is cold, hard and heavy ... avant-garde, experimental, noisy ...

made with steel, bits of pipeline from my maternal great-great uncle, Canadian pioneer of the gas industry, a bow from his daughter the violinist, a piano key from her daughter the classical pianist, jangling with a typewriter's key from my paternal grandfather, from his typewriter factory, cardboard from his first "suitcase," an anxious bundle tossed toward the American dream, edged with fur from my maternal grandmother's mink coat stitched with red cloth from my paternal grandmother's scarf she used to keep her hair from falling forward in the typewriter factory and pink silk from my paternal great aunt, from her hat factory

I reach for more Lithuanian ancestors and cousins across the Atlantic Ocean, for their long unchartered names, still mostly unintelligible, for Lithuanian genealogists to help me root myself in this new global home....

pointillistic, traditional

dots on the world map, birth places, ports of entry, churches, funeral parlors, burial grounds ...

uploading documents, returning Anglicized names to their original forms, adding notes to records, responding to scandal, ambiguous lineage, a great-great grandfather sired by a noble, born before wedlock, given his mother's name, recovering his title, our Lithuanian name Nagrodskė

heroic

I sew a metal heraldic shield into the quilt.

When We'll Worship Jesus[1]

We'll worship jesus / When jesus do / Somethin'
—Amiri Baraka

We'll worship Jesus
when he doesn't just lie there
a babe in a manger playing with his mother's locks and breasts
When he doesn't display himself naked nailed to a cross
wearing only white underpants and a crown of thorns
trying to attract female admirers and move them to pity
When he doesn't choose to honor only one woman, Mary
        Magdalene
who kissed his feet
When he cares more about nature and earthly creatures
instead of crying in his manger and disturbing sheep and cattle
or with Moses setting fire to a bush
and not checking what life dwelled within
When he doesn't cause ecological discord and let Moses part
        the Red Sea
or take all the fish from hungry sea creatures for his friends
When he speaks out about child abuse
and doesn't let Abraham try to kill and terrorize his son
When he doesn't deny and dishonor his earthly father
and say he was created by something hollow in the sky
raging on the cross and shouting that his father has
        abandoned him
When he doesn't deny healthy sexuality and refuse to date

---

1. This poem was inspired by and is a response to Amiri Baraka's poem
"When We'll Workship Jesus"

or use Mary Magdalene as a cover for his relationship with
        Judas
whose public kiss got him arrested
When he doesn't turn water into wine at a wedding
after people had drunk enough and promote alcoholism
When he doesn't afflict people and then save their lives
to make others think he is powerful
When he doesn't afflict and then save himself
to make people think he is not from planet earth

English Class 101

I am tired of the copying and pasting
human disconnection, disrespect, the absence of thought
Some students now weeks into the course still don't know my
     name, course title
essays purchased from Course Hero, Grade Fixer
extra time of work for investigation of academic violations
I finally found the essay four students used—my unnatural
     glee
I imagine myself in uniform with a bright gold badge
What are the differences between an instructor and a
     detective?

In class I give the students each a piece of white paper
and tell them to write about how a personal narrative makes
     their lives feel more meaningful and to share a
     personal experience of struggle

The white paper extends across the class like a blanket of
     snow
thoughts cascade down, striking the page
each thought stepping slowly falling deeply after the next
     toward me

I hold gently each piece of paper
stare into each human face … happy, sad, peaceful, angry,
     anxious, tired
examining the script, pencil lines scratching out words
some words underlined, circled

upright slant, backward slant, forward slant, slippery slope
small spaces between words, larger spaces
thin, wide, tall, short, round, angular, sharp
All words in capitals, heavy black marker, big I's, small i's
I's dotted with hearts, red heart doodles, a first name
     highlighted with turquoise marker
flower doodles with purple and neon yellow marker
"Maria & Santiago are [something in Spanish]"
the words "I love this pen"

CYNTHIA LEE STEELE

To Scream the Impossible Scream

To dream the impossible dream
To fight the unbeatable foe
To bear with unbearable sorrow
To run where the brave dare not go
    —Joe Darion, "The Impossible Dream"

Scream; just try to scream. All that emits is air.

A whooshing sound like brakes on a train or a city bus when someone pulls the cord, complete with the screech at the end. Like a cop show when some almost imperceptible whoosh and screech is heard in the background. They all scratch their heads, and Bailey says,

"I swear I've heard that noise before ..."

And they all find the kidnapped child just in time. "He's still got a pulse, Jim!"

But, I swear, there were times when my own pulse grew faint, and I imagined how they would find me too late. Because I hadn't been kidnapped. Because my abuser lived in our home. We fed him and laughed with him. I ran away. Until I learned that cops will always bring you back. And, I learned, for so long, that to scream would not matter, even if I could.

After high school, at 17, I called my "real" father. After not seeing or hearing from him in many years, I asked if I could join him in Sitka, Alaska—about as far away as Seattle is from Anchorage. He worked at Sheldon Jackson College as part of the administrative staff as head groundskeeper. When I told him where I was—I'd hitched a ride 500 miles from Big Lake to Fairbanks with a friend—he gave me the 'vagabond' lecture, again. I thought: We barely know each other. But, I was desperate. I promised to be on the honor roll and not embarrass him—him, "a faculty member," he said. "A faculty member," I acknowledged. I'd be a faculty member's kid. The bar was high. I never felt I could do it. But, I had nothing to lose but time.

At Sheldon Jackson, I took acting and English classes, there on the water on the most beautiful place I'd ever seen, this Sitka island of islands. During the days, I chatted up James A. Michener as he worked on his book *Alaska*. On the weekends, I binge drank, danced at the local bars—the Shee Atiká or Kiksadi—with a fake ID, and passed out in the arms of any boy who wouldn't take advantage of me, often after dramatically quoting Steinbeck or Shakespeare:

> When, in disgrace with fortune and
> men's eyes, I all alone beweep my outcast
> state,

In short, they tolerated me.

In acting classes during the week, I worked hard, but I often froze on stage. I also froze in life. I froze many times and for reasons I could not explain; I no longer even tried. I just rode it out.

In one of my best moments, I played the part of Ariel to the director's Sebastian.

Pointing, I declared:

> You are three men of sin ... you 'mongst men
> Being most unfit to live. I have made you mad;

By "his Sebastian," I mean a famous visiting director, actor, playwright from New York whose name is now gone to me. No matter how I opened the door to this man for advances (he was quite handsome and I was quite young), he never showed me anything but kindness in his eyes; he never pushed me away. Rather, he focused on the lines we said. And we said them at the college, at old folks' homes, and on any stage in that tiny town that would have us. He focused on the parts we played. The lives we stepped into.

In class, he asked me, one day, to do the impossible.

Not just me—everyone. But it was as if I had been alone on stage. He asked me—us—to scream. My head got all swimmy and I asked to be excused. I puked in the echoey bathroom with the clear block windows up high and the ivory everything. The sound of retching I'd gotten used to, being, as I'd name later, bulimic. But, this was something else. Still, it was a purging. A cathartic form of emesis. Like releasing the Devil himself. Followed, almost instantly, by a massive migraine. They'd been with me for years, these blinding headaches, coming on strongly at the first sign of stress.

After headache and vomiting from the migraine that lasted for the usual three days, I returned to class, hoping the "screaming" request had passed.

"We held off the exercise," the room boomed, "until you were well enough to join us."

"The fuck," I muttered under my breath and feared the director heard.

"What?" a peer asked.

"I'm in Hell," I said. Some laughed.

I admitted, "I can't do it. I could never scream. Even when I should scream, nothing comes out." Acid filled my stomach. I overshared again. I made a mental note not to elaborate.

The director's dark head of hair turned toward me, and his eyes accepted my words as a challenge, of the acting sort.

"Use that. Yes, good. Use those memories, that energy, to push the scream out!"

The rapes came back. The first when I was 11. Then, the attempted rapes of my stepfather and his best friend that lasted for years. I'd fought back and run away.

I vomited in my mouth a little, then swallowed it. I stared at the director, my jaw grimacing, my eyes glazing over.

"Right now, what's happening?" he asked. Then, seeing my fear, he said quickly, "No, wait, don't answer that. Just 'think' where you are, what's around you, who's there, and SCREAM!"

Air seeped slowly from my chest as I stood on that large auditorium's creaky stage. The noise was barely audible, even in this cavernous space where we all wore socks or tights to avoid making any noise.

"Good," he said. He passed to the next person. *Thank God, that's over. I won't have to be tortured at this game that I cannot win,* I thought.

The class became funny with my classmates' huge screams and laughs. The director looked at me like all was groovy in every way. Then, he returned to me abruptly and barked, "CINDY, SCREAM!"

I wanted to. I relaxed one fraction of an iota, purposefully, and my voice came out in fits and starts. Like a baby donkey learning to bray. Like a woman strangled.

"Better. You're getting there."

I felt lightheaded, but not like puking. I guessed that was progress. I looked around the room and thought, No one knows. No one knows my private hell. Why can't I yell?

Years of conditioning. A hand over my mouth and eyes while he took my virginity. Immobile muteness. No one knows this.

117

The director went around the room again, then just like before, stopped on me.

"I did it already," I said.

The eyes around me looked confused. Had I not? I thought I had screamed. "Let's do another exercise," he said. "A body relaxation, then try it."

He was genius at getting us silly, flopping around, forgetting ourselves, and laughing. "Now, Cindy, SCREAM!" He called out. "Scream for all you're worth! Scream for every reason you've ever had to scream. No air, just volume, and GO!"

A shriek the likes of which I'd only heard once came out. The gargling, watery scream of the first shark attack victim of *Jaws*.

I kept screaming as directed, "From your feet to the top of your head, let it out!"

The shriek of a young Fay Wray, her blood curdling, long wails, head thrown back, arms wildly flailing at the creature King Kong. What seemed about 15 minutes later, my throat hurt, and wet tears fell from my chin.

I looked up, and heard the clapping of my classmates. The look of pride on the director's face. And I was free.

Dancing Queen, Young and Sweet

Ooh, you can dance
Ooh, you can dance
You can jive
Having the time of your life
Ooh, see that girl
Watch that scene
Digging the dancing queen
    —Benny Andersson, Björn Ulvaeus and Stig Anderson,
"Dancing Queen"

Dancing was a big part of my growing up. I wanted to grand jeté ("large throw") my body in the high jump of a ballet dancer. I wanted to do the catlike strut of a jazz dancer. I yearned to "Do the Hustle" in 1975 with Van McCoy. My sister and I would practice doing the Bump all the way down to the ground in quick hip hits, bouncing at each hit of the bump. We'd launch our arms up into the letters of the YMCA. But only I was brave enough to do the Funky Chicken, to point my Disco Finger to the sky, or to do the jerky staccato movements of the Robot.

I wanted my body to be good, to bend to my will and not the will of others. I wanted my body to be free. I'd gone to ballet as a small child—lovely that my mother or my stepfather, or whoever put me in that class did so, because I felt like one of them, if only for the class period. I felt what I imagined other kids felt like while dancing in the basement, surrounded by ballet bars.

It was glorious, this feeling of sameness: same stockings, same ballet shoes, same slim bodies. We looked like children together. Not at all like what I'd become. I'd come to think of

119

myself as growing into womanhood already because he kept touching me—my mother's new boyfriend, brushing against me.

I didn't feel weirdness there at all. I didn't even think of him while listening to the same music danced to by Mikhail Baryshnikov. We did the big lunges and went up on our toes and moved our hands out and low and leapt through the air like nimble deer, sure-footed.

I danced timidly because it was new. And no, I probably can't tell you all the positions, not without cheating, and I'm not cheating writing this. I just remember the names had such beautiful sounds. I moved my legs like scissors across the room, flew through the air, the breeze glanced my cheeks, and I landed just so.

I wanted to be dancing forever. But ballet lasted, of course, only for a short time because we moved again. That time when we did ballet would be eclipsed but not forgotten. I would take that memory and meld it into different areas of my life.

I started dancing again as a bubble gummer at teen clubs in Anchorage by age 10, 11, dancing my heart out to the Bee Gees, KC and the Sunshine Band, to the Rick Dees and his Cast of Idiots, confidently belting out their song "Disco Duck."

> All of a sudden, I began to change
> I was on the dance floor acting strange
> (Quack, quack, quack, quack)
> Flapping my arms, I began to cluck
> (Quack, quack)
> Look at me, I'm the disco duck

I wasn't just having fun. I disappeared inside this Dancing Queen character. Past—forgotten. Present moment—accelerated, like a fast car. Still, I felt different than many of the other kids. They wanted to be cool. They wanted to be liked. I was never so sure I was still likable. I wanted to be the perfect dancer, and then, I thought, maybe they might.

I needed to be the "It" girl: Hair like Dorothy Hamill—a short wedge, a pixie. Ma's hairstylist friend, Lynn, did it for free, or, more likely, in trade for weed. I loved Lynn for it, Lynn whose son Keegan we also loved but we didn't see either of them after this time. I loved my hair's new movement—its swish. I related to Annette's life in the movie *Saturday Night Fever*. She gets violated in the back seat of a car then watches a guy jump off a bridge. I'd already been violated. I kept dancing. Hoping for better. Accepting what was. Happily, I did feel I was running part of my life, making things happen.

At underage dance clubs, I did more watching at times than dancing. I watched how people's bodies moved. I tested to see if my body would comply with the movements, and it often would. I memorized patterns. I'd watch *Saturday Night Fever*; my sister and I went to the movies frequently. Mama's Daddy had been a projectionist in South Dakota, so she saw the importance of us going to movies as a kid, which we often did by ourselves. If there were dance scenes in the movies, I paid close attention, even stepping to the aisle to repeat them immediately.

Because I was/am dyslexic, I had to do it a thousand times—memorize patterns—until it became one piece. This to my sister's annoyance, which I often ignored or pretended to. I had done the same repetitions in ballet and made it all one with that teacher whose thin sweater was tied at her side, with a wrap-around skirt, and those magic legs. Her hair tucked just so into a tight bun.

Yes, those were the legs I wanted. I put my order in. I remember looking for where my belly button rested next to my sisters in the tiny, slim bathroom mirror. I have this elongated torso and poor, dwarfed legs that look wonderful only when I sit down. A slick illusion could be created if I wore Mama's stacked tennies that tied.

The dancing never left my mind. By 10, I could do the Bump, the Funky Chicken, the Bus Stop, the Robot, and the YMCA. These moves, these beats, became something I could depend on. We changed locations, but the dance steps never changed. By 13, I could do the Hustle, partner dancing with spin upon spin and linkups with a partner who had to be— and was—on cue. When I heard music—thump, thump—it became my music. It became part of my repertoire, part of my collection of special moves. I knew one day I would have time on stage when I would be the only thing anyone would look at. I would be a star.

I prepared for that moment. I got to know music, going to the DJs at the radio station, talking to them about music as a tween, wanting to know specifically which songs were the great dance songs, building my collection of cool music, which I would then win through dance contests at underage clubs that I frequented. That was my personal education.

I've no idea if my sister shared my craze, but I didn't notice her being so into dance. I obsessed about dancing. I felt nothing but death could keep me from it.

I could say I got it from my mama. Mama would go out dancing. I would watch her dress up when I was six and seven years old. She wore this pink Pepto-Bismol–shade dress, with sequins and a deep slit up the sides. I waited for the day to come when I would be invited to wear that dress, with rhinestones trimming the edges. I imagined flipping my wrist in a turn and having the bottom of the dress flip outward.

Later, the dress I stood to inherit was gone. We'd moved Anchorage to Wasilla, 50 miles away. But, in Wasilla, there was still a teen nightclub, and I was young, 12 to 14.

The junior high had a record player, and that record player belonged to the school. I considered it mine and would play music at lunchtime and get everyone dancing. There were people who thought it was the loserliest thing, so not-for-this-age-group. They thought I was fast. I heard that word a few times. But I wanted to dance, and I did dance. I liked to dance fast.

I went to two junior highs. One of them was a disaster in Anchorage and the one in Wasilla a triumph and perhaps a failure for so many reasons. But mostly, there was dancing at the kid club, the late-night teen dance hall in Wasilla. The boys there were two to four years older than me: Carl Nevada—tall, dark, and handsome, Mitch Rivard, blond and pale, both sports stars who could dance, growing into men. They chose me as a "kid" because of my dance skills, their own girlfriends looking on with what I imagined as a sadness that I bested them and was chosen. They had to choose me to win. Their drive to win was as strong as mine.

Those boys wore the white suits of *Saturday Night Fever*. I looked up to them, and by up, I mean a foot up. They were so tall. I wore instead of that pink Pepto Bismol dress, a pink Lemay number I donned until it frayed threadbare.

I took that dancing to high school. I took it to the Christian school where I would sneak away from that life to dance the dances all night until it was over. People spoke about me, not about my parents who sold weed etc., but of my dance skills. I was rising like cream to the top. Once in a while, I made out with a boy outside, and I took a break. But really, I just wanted a break from all that mashing.

I was always one of the last to leave. I saw how people were hooking up there. I saw how people were into the coolness. They were doing drugs, and I did a bit of the drinking and sometimes other stuff, but I wanted to be sharp enough to dance. And win contests.

MARTHA KAPLAN

Birth-days for baby boomers

taken squalling
from the birth room

on carts wheeled to the end
of long halls far

from mothers' rooms,
kept separate for 24 hours

to let mothers rest
in hospitals designed for free

by producers of formulas
who knew well their business,

and nurses taught to put babies
directly to nipples, touch cheeks

so baby would turn away
and nurses would say

to new mothers living far from
their own mothers

how sorry they are that baby
has rejected the breast—

shaky beginnings for both baby
and mother, me, and mine.

For Days of Auld Lang Syne

here is the song
that couldn't be sung
on the night [after]
on the day of the
transformation of you,
my friend [my mistake]
to [you] abductor

here is the song
for the cross-town careen,
for the car and its parts,
with my hand on the handle
of the unclosed door

here is a song
for me who jumped
from the car
when you slowed,
when you left me
in the midnight dark

here is a song
for the wheels of the car
and the jolt of the bump
that you hit
that you thought
was my body

and here is a song
for the houses
all closed in the dark
and the people
with guns by their beds

and here is a song
for the fear that resides
in the night of the long
walk home

and here [old friend]
is the rage that
follows the fear

and here is the scar
that remains

Her Inner Child Loves the Wildness

She loves to walk. She is often sad. In her loneliness she walks along her rustic road, cuts down to the one below the hill through the grassy easement created for underground electricity, and walks all the way to the steep cliff above the railroad tracks that run along the shores of Puget Sound. She climbs a madrone that hangs over the side, hugs it, watches the water. A deserted horse barn sits along the road. She loves the smell of it, old hay, and grass weeds. Sometimes she shelters there in the rain. She can tell when spring is on the way, the raindrops are no longer sharp against the face, and there is the soft smell to the Chinook air in the rain. She loves to walk in the rain. No one bothers her. She can wander as she pleases.

this empty page before me

stymies the breach from brain to heart to hand,
    I can't breathe, can't breathe,
    my eyes fuzz, fingers ache for words—

    what blank rancor, what pique, what grudge, ruptures
you,
        word-hoard?
        Break! And give leave!

Set me a seining net to draw a couple-colored word from out
    the River Lethe
wind me a path along the Welkin Way, let me
    see a sea of words wend their way away, let me
        wail song along the Wendell sea

and send me sails to cross the old Whale Road in ships
to harpoon ancient words, set them in baskets made of reeds,
lay them at crossroads so travelers and traders in words
    can span the breach, never starve for lack
        of wind-eyes for breath
        to write a brindled page

Across the Missouri Breaks
for my son

When I was a fisher boy,
I sang beside a pond on a high prairie
where the sky burned above
and clouds owned the land.

When I was a fisher boy,
in a yellow hat and yellow boots
I held star dust and lime from
ancient bones; time clothed me silver.

When I was a fisher boy,
I flew over continents, soaring over mountains
to the sea, traversing desert buttes and red stone
of carved cliffs, seeking roots of curves
in algorithms both wise and true.

Night rides on blue roads east of Austin

crackled tongues of vitreous
brains female my absent mind
roving through dirty-sock K-Marts
whirling with surreptitious

gun-racked landscapes wracked
gauzy with ruined teachers
and gangly piney woods echoing
phallus thoughts that ricochet

holy, holy, wholly lost souls
picnic-tabling ice-house nights
with fisty throats slinging
plastic wrapped nostalgia

that croaks in Llano-lifted heat
bloody with clandestine couplings
hanging on starry-stranded hopes
that Spanish the mosses off gnarly

shadows of old live oaks beside
two-lane asphalts wheeling over
ghost-hosts of ancient footpaths
gulfing from glasslands to the shill

country conjuring psilocybin visions
of losing my way along the Brazos

LARISSA SHMAILO

Interview

My autobiography will read: *I am hired*. But no: I am still here, in this little office, where the fluorescent light surrounds me like cloacal fluid. The personnel manager's eyes are dark and dilated, without visible irises, whether from the peculiar quanta of the overhead light or the cocaine of my need, I don't know.

She is self-satisfied and content now, self-consciously busy, and she preens herself with papers on her desk. She is almost ready to talk to me. I wait like a dog who has not been walked for a long time.

Finally, she turns her attention to me. Why do you want this job? she asks.

I'm desperate, I reply. My unemployment checks ran out two weeks ago and I have no money. I've been on unemployment a lot these last few years and I have no reserves; in all senses of the word, I have no reserves left. You see, I have a manic-depressive illness, a very severe one, not just a few mood swings here or there, or a common-cold-type depression, but grand mal mania with delusions, and I've lost a lot of jobs. I don't get fired per se—they just eliminate my position, and this way, they don't get sued. But I did sue one place, not for firing me because I was a manic-depressive, but because I was a manic-depressive. Is there a difference? I don't know.

I got unemployment that time, and then again when I danced over where the AIDS orphans were buried. I was coming late because I had to dervish over their corpses, the corpses of unburied dead. I was dancing to mark the spot. Perhaps, I thought, perhaps, they would see and understand, but they fired me. I was coming in late a lot. They eliminated my position—they were glad to give me unemployment. Really, they would have done a lot more just to be rid of me.

I take medication now. It makes me slow, but I can still do this work. Not with any enthusiasm—I am no longer sharp. I'm burnt out, as you can imagine, from so many illnesses. Sometimes my thinking is fuzzy, and I simply don't have the fire any more. I used to be quite good, quite an overachiever. I worked long hours and slaved to make everything perfect. Now, I just rewrite the old. It's all old.

With supervision, I know I will be okay. I'm hoping for a boss who is indecisive and a little lazy, and if we can pass letters back and forth for endless time-consuming corrections, it wouldn't bother me at all. That would be just fine. Bureaucracy and indecision used to bother me, I worried about my brilliant career and how the slowness and incompetence and stupidity of my boss would hold me back, but then I became a poet and didn't give a shit anymore. I once cared passionately about poetry, too, but now I don't worry about that much, either. I just want a paycheck and a place to go during the day so I don't crawl into bed and piss on the sheets.

You know, a job like this one wasn't good enough for me once, but now this really is the best I can do. I would be delighted if I got this job. If I could do it. If I could show up. If I don't just crawl back into bed. But you see I live entirely on the charity of my mother. The alimony runs out soon. I was always so confident, confident in my ability to take care of myself, to come back from any disaster. That's gone now, you understand, completely, utterly gone.... I used to think I could change the world; now, I don't think I can change my sheets....

But I'm pretty sure I can still do this job, as long as I don't have to create anything. If I can copy a template, I know I'll do fine. I was once creative; I was a bright, no, brilliant kid, but I drank a lot, spent a lot of time on psych wards, and it started to catch up with me. There's only so many times you can get really manic before the permanent damage sets in. Anyway, my psychiatrist says I need some structure, and I agree, and a job would really help.

Does that answer your question? You know, your pupils are so dilated. It's an interview, a two-way street. Have you seen into me? I can't see into you. Maybe you're a manic-depressive, too. Maybe you rush out from here every day to the office of a waiting shrink to weep and scream your despair, to say, I can't go on, it hurts too much....

I see your irises now, blue like mine, and know you have lived without sickness and without despair, and your normal life of normal frustrations and no huge events looks at me without a trace of pity. This interview and our interaction is the worst thing that will happen to you this month. I know you've had your troubles, too. It's just that I have to come back from a place that doesn't even exist to sit here today, and I'm so tired I could just die. If I could do it, I would, but I'm afraid to jump and the pills just don't work. I know, I've tried a dozen times.

If this were the thirties, you would give me a break. Back then, no one pretended that things were just fine. People liked homeless people, called them hoboes, gave them jobs. I gave my diamond engagement ring to a homeless man last year, I gave all my clothes away to the poor, because I was confident back then. Do you know what I would do for one ounce of confidence today?

I stopped and the fluorescence ate my words. The papers on her desk absorbed the sounds, and around me like sewage my cheerful interview-self returned, and I answered the other questions as anybody would, and she pretended that she hadn't heard a word of what I had said.

Fitness

The definition of *fitness* in genetics is to reproduce successfully. I have no genetic fitness. I did once: my genetic material was carried by my sister's daughter, my godchild and niece, Irene, whom I raised and let down. She committed suicide at the age of 35. She was a psychiatrist who knew pharmacology well and a determined individual who said that if she were to kill herself, she would do it so that no one would know. And so she did.

As a young woman, I seemed to want to get pregnant pretty badly. I had many boyfriends and did not use birth control. Mentally ill and quite alcoholic, I had three abortions, two by a kind, brilliant father and one by either of two men, a pockmarked writer or a mediocre bassist. It never occurred to me to tell the kind, brilliant father, with whom I had a long-term relationship, about the pregnancies; my mother said he would not want to know and I accepted that. It turned out she was right.

I had a complete nervous breakdown at the time of my third abortion, with a vivid hallucination of a brown, curly-headed fetus, the subject of my poem "Abortion Hallucination":

Abortion Hallucination

A vision of a snake with glowing red eyes
formed by the light of   garbage trucks and   screeching new cars
driven by men who had once   bought me dinner
then hated me when I didn't want to fuck them twice.

Carlight passing late at night on a street of an ugly
precinct lying deceiving the unwary who think it leads home

It is late so dark it is almost light   that time of night when
the light hits the metal and the glass of summer windows left ajar
make me want something   someone   I don't know who

The metal gate to the yard refracts this message via Queens boys who
drive too fast too late at night   refracts this message to the
window   where
I watch from the couch

In the corner of the basement where my father used to lie I

Watch, interested, as the snake
grows larger and more menacing   I am
taken slightly aback but remember him   remember that I like
handling snakes   and smile
and as always he softens   grows smaller
becomes a hippopotamus   I have won again   I have stared him
down
made him warm
and the Nile gives up its life to me
animals carnivorous and calm   come home to me
two by two

I watch for the longest time
until the largest fills the window with his face
black as light
Agnus Dei

for this man's baby for   this man's   baby for this man's baby
came the flood.

I contented myself with being my niece's crazy aunt, and she
idolized me as a child. Later, as she saw my feet of clay, the hero
worship ended and she became more distant, going about med
school and being married and becoming rich. Around then, in
my thirties, sober and functioning on a successful med combo,

I saw I might have the chance not to totally wreck a poor child's life. I had an intense desire to have a child. The problem was that I would need to come off my teratogenic medications. I tried: I was stark raving mad for three years until I finally gave up the idea.

I became more committed and involved as a poet and sublimated my reproductive instincts. And there was still my niece, brilliant and successful. Until the call in the middle of the night in October sixteen years ago from my sister: "Lora, Irene is dead." Dead. I was sober and I couldn't smoke, but my sister and I hit every IHOPS in the suburbs of San Francisco, eating ourselves into a coma during the funeral and the wake. I gained 50 pounds that autumn.

My pen doesn't flow for Irene—the ink drips slowly and meagerly, like clotted blood. I am aware that I am not her mother and don't have a mother's right to grieve. But I can still feel her tiny hands pulling on the hairs of my arms as I cradled her infant form to sleep, can remember baptizing her, remember telling her the plot of *Hamlet* when she was five, watching her read all of Dickens (why Dickens?), hearing her call out "help me, Mama!" during a brutal depression, seeing the cut marks on her teenaged wrists.

Aerial View of the Rockies

The gods like to trace their fingers in the world;
like leaves from a primordial tree, landforms
bare their veins. Clever of her to suicide this way
leaving no one but me to know. Impassive as
the dead face she wanted no one to see, clouds
hide rigor in the lines, purposeful or not, below.
In winter, sunrise looks like sunset in this distant
land, soon to be nearer, nearer, soon.

Near the end of her life, my mother, given to bursts of anger, carefully prepared and delivered a measured speech to me and my sister, to each of us separately. She quietly and sincerely stated that if she had it to do over, she would not have had children. It was important to her that her daughters know this. I thought for a moment that perhaps she was consoling me for my childlessness, but that would have been another woman, not my Mama.

I have no nuclear family now—Mama, Papa, my sister Tamara, and my niece and godchild Irene are dead. I quickly sold the family home last year, but am haunted by it in my dreams. And I have no fitness, no genetic material except my cousins' daughters, bright, pretty, too distant for me to care. I have buried everyone, and have no one to bury me; I counted on Irene for that, and she would have done me proud. But I suppose when the time comes, I won't be in the condition to mind.

Madwoman

Here I am again walking among these vague and tepid people they evoke a slight feeling of distaste in me they smell my pain they have no idea I just hold my phone the cellular phone I use for a disguise and I talk, talk to the ultimate answering service I walk and I talk to God

When you died I ripped the electrodes out of my skull and ran away from the land of cables and TV sets great battles of television were fought here great battles were lost Soho is no different from uptown or downtown it's all money and talking and bars sex and cars job job job so I went to see the trees

The trees were luminous the leaves forming patterns of light on the ground and as the light played on my hair and my cheeks I realized that no one ever dies they just become trees even Marilyn Monroe was alive in a leaf I saw for an instant your face all aquiver in the shaking of a fern in the light of the wind and I kissed the trees so I knew you were not dead not really you would not be so cruel as to die really die

Under the West Side Highway I met all the men who lived there and one girl she was 22 and pregnant and had AIDS I didn't stay long but I stayed long enough under the West Side Highway I slept with Jesus in a cap talked madman Spanish with Tito and the dirty apostles knew there would always be enough loaves and fishes for me knew that no matter how hard it got I would always be safe and held near close to God it was my destiny to be greatly loved

I chose then to be close to God to throw away my clothing and be close to God there were times when not even a shirt came between me and God

Under the West Side Highway I spoke to Jesus his face always changing now Alex who lived in a tent near the wall now Panama drinking wine now Juan in his tin and cardboard hut

You followed me watched me you were worried how would I get home and back to the life I had known and I said look who's talking you died after all it's hardly for you to criticize me if I go off the beaten path a little too

And as for the others they worried too unknown to them the protection that I had and had always had I said to them all don't worry I will love you pray you home look can't you see….I am your guardian angel and you thought I was just homeless and mad as though God hadn't made the whole world just for me

Well now I am cured I go to the bank I take pills I sit in restaurants have a job I worry about money and whether my new boyfriend has AIDs we don't even have sex he's too busy with his job it's just as well none of these men have anything that would compel you or keep you through the night its just banging bones after all

You see very few men have souls and very few men have courage the few who have the courage to follow their souls are mostly all dead lost in leaves people kill them you know I don't know any more I take pills and talk into the cellular phone sometimes I think I hear your voice sometimes I think I hear you and then no it's just the pills I get a hum in my ear its not you I know you are not dead but you're not here either and I miss you

I am cured so they say but you can't really ever take the gift of madness away once you have been stripped by God of everything clothing family freedom senses you are his for life and I was stripped oh yes dear lord of everything every last thing God took everything leaving only my soul but I found that was enough

And you you people think you have things but really the next breath you take is the only thing you have so how different are you from me

Look at us again we the homeless and see us for who we are the archangels of God

You can not take the gift of madness away I will always know about trees will always see the arch of my lover's neck in the patterns of their light I will know that the patch of sky between the birch tree and the willow is him his azure face and I will always hear the voice of God wherever I go no pill can block him out no TV set can drown his voice no fool can block the face of God from me

Look at me madwoman I am Magdalene I am Joan of Arc I am St. Marilyn Monroe and I will always be your angel baby I will always be your saint pray to me.

Biographical Notes

Larissa Shmailo (Editor) is the author of two novels and six poetry collections, most recently *Dora/Lora*, about the role of Ukrainian kapos in the Holocaust. Her poetry album *Exorcism* won the New Century Best Spoken Word album award. Larissa's work has appeared in over 30 anthologies, including *Measure for Measure: An Anthology of Poetic Meters* (Penguin Random House), *Words for the Wedding* (Penguin), and *Contemporary Russian Poetry* (Dalkey). Larissa is the original English-language translator of the first Futurist opera *Victory over the Sun*, performed at the Los Angeles County Museum of Art, the Garage Museum of Moscow, the Brooklyn Academy of Music, and theaters and universities worldwide. Larissa also edited the anthology *Twenty-First Century Russian Poetry*. She has been teaching the Writing Resilience workshop for people affected by trauma, addiction, and/or mental illness since 2020; new this year is her Formal Poetry workshop. Larissa also provides one-on-one writing coaching. Larissa attributes her recovery from mental illness to the practice and communities of writing.

Rachel Blum is the author of *The Doctor of Flowers*—a book of poems reflecting the loss of her eldest daughter to pediatric cancer—published in 2018 by 3: A Taos Press. Her second book of poems, *Talisman*, is available online as a free e-book on her poetry website, **rachelblumpoetry.com**. She has taught creative writing in mental health and hospital settings.

William Considine was born in McKeesport. PA. He obtained higher education on scholarships and work-study. He graduated "With Great Distinction" from Stanford and cum laude from Harvard Law School. He was first encouraged to write poetry by Diane Middlebrook at Stanford and first formally studied writing poetry at Harvard with Elizabeth Bishop. Bill was a member of the playwrights workshop of the Public Theater, coordinated by Ed Bullins, with four staged readings there. He presented his plays in performances at Theater for the New City, La Mama, Brooklyn

Army Terminal, Limbo Lounge, Ear Inn, ABC No Rio, and Dixon Place. He writes poems and plays. His books include *The Furies* and *Strange Coherence* (both from *The Operating System*), *The Other Myrtle* (Finishing Line Press), and *Continent of Fire* (Kelsay Books). His full-length plays *Moral Support* and *Women's Mysteries* were presented in New York City in 2019 to critical praise. His recent short verse plays include *Aunt Peg and the Comptometer*, at Bowery Poetry Club in 2020; *Persephone's Return*, *Odyssey's End*, *John Milton in the Tower*, and *A Common Tongue*, all on Zoom during the covid pandemic; and *Over Drinks* and *Oedipus in Love* at Polaris North, NYC, in 2023. A retired lawyer, he previously served as a lecturer in law at Pace Law School, an administrative law judge for the City of New York, a City administrator, an arbitrator, and as vice president of a public service corporation.

Paula Curci, Nassau County Poet Laureate Emeritus 2022–2024, produces *Calliope's Corner* and *What's The Buzz*® on WRHU. She is a poet correspondent for THE SCENE and a certified Journal to the Self™ writing instructor. Under the Acoustic Poets Network™ brand she's produced *Emissary*, *Bittersweet* and *Done That Poetry and Posics*™-The Audio Version. The APN Visitation Project also produces community engagement poetry events like the SCR-NYSCA grant awarded Word Festival, in Oceanside NY, and the Poetry: It's a 'Shore' Thing! Festival, in Long Beach NY. Paula spearheads the Shore Poets open mic and the free verse workshops at the Long Beach Library, Hicksville Library's open mic, and Port Washington Library's poetry reading circle. She's co-edited *Poetry: It's a Shore Thing! in an Unsure World: An Anthology of Micro Memoirs from the South Shore Poets of Long Island* and has written several chapbooks. You can find her work on Soundcloud and Amazon.

Dennis Formento lives in Slidell, Louisiana, USA, near his native New Orleans. His books of poetry include *Spirit Vessels* (FootHills Publishing, 2018) *Looking for An Out Place* (FootHills, 2010,) and *Cineplex* (Paper Press, 2014.) He edited *Mesechabe: The Journal of Surregionalism*, 1991–2001. He has collaborated locally with musicians including his own Frank Zappatistas free jazz/free verse project, and in Italy with the renowned "avant-folk" group Duo Bottasso. He has organized readings for the world-wide network 100,000 Poets for Change in New Orleans and St. Tammany Parish, L.A., since 2011. In 2023 he won the poetry category of the Wisdom-Faulkner literary competition with his manuscript *Phaeton's Wheels*.

Anna Fridlis is a memoirist, poet and essayist based in Newark, NJ on indigenous Lenape land. She lives and writes at the intersection of multiple identities: Jewish, Soviet immigrant, white, disabled, neurodivergent, and queer. Her work addresses the impact of intergenerational trauma on the trajectory of a life, tracking trauma's creeping effects on mental and physical health, family relationships, creative output, and the scope of the imagination. Anna's work captures one version of a Soviet Jewish immigrant story that both faces its utter devastation and searches for answers and deep healing in self expression, nature, and somatics. Anna teaches first year writing at Parsons the New School for Design and cohabits with her bunny Willow, who also happens to be her muse.

Iris Gersh grew up in the Shawangunks. She lived in Boston where she received a B.A. from B.U; at the Magic Tortoise 20 miles north of Taos during the seventies; in south Florida; in Korinthos, Greece; and since 2005, Albuquerque, loving the High Desert life. She has her MFA in Creative Writing from Florida International University. She taught Sociology and English Composition classes at Brookline College and CNM. Much of her last fifteen years' work was in the field of editing and proofreading. Iris's poems and stories are published in national and local literary magazines and anthologies, including *Packinghouse Review; Alembic; Manzano Mountain Review;* and yearly and quarterly *Fixed and Free Anthologies*. A pre-pandemic highlight was being Feature Poet at Chatter Sunday's 600th Show in March 2020. Soon after, she dwelled in a bubble with her Mainekoon Chico, leading to post-pandemic ups and downs. Her poetry book *A Thousand Questions* was published by Finishing Line Press in December 2020. Since December of 2021, Iris joined the writing group Writing Resilience, where she listens to and shares her writing with a group of supportive, brilliant writers.

Nina Glueckselig is an inveterate New Yorker despite time spent living in Boston and San Francisco. She has always loved to write and has journalled since the third grade. She studied fiction writing with Frank Bergon at Vassar College and attended Luis Urrea's creative writing class through Harvard University's Continuing Education program. She has attended Larissa Shmailo's Writing Resilience workshop since 2020. This has enabled her to complete pieces like "Apple of My Eye," "Crack in a Rock," "Grapefruit and Coleslaw" and many others, all with a view towards completing a memoir. Every week there is a new prompt to write about, and it is very effective in looking at one's life and processing trauma. Her writing deals with her experience as a child of Holocaust survivors. Writing about the sensuous beauty of gemstones, jewelry and clothing, she also explores her experiences with depression.

Martha Jackson Kaplan is a recipient of the Zylpha Mapp Robinson International Poetry Award and two Editor-in-Chief Awards from *Möbius the Poetry Magazine*. She won both a first and a third place in the Poets' Choice Contest from the Wisconsin Fellowship of Poets. She holds degrees in sociology and art history from the University of Houston and has done post grad work in English at University of Wisconsin–Madison. She also holds an M.Ed. from Loyola of Chicago, with credentials in Special Ed. and English from Edgewood College. She is a retired teacher who was raised in Seattle, has lived in both Houston and Chicago, and now lives in Madison, Wisconsin. Publications can be found in *Cirque: A Literary Journal for the North Pacific Rim, Hummingbird, The Night Heron Barks, Unlikely Stories,* including the 20th Anniversary Issue, *Verse Wisconsin, Wisconsin Poets' Calendar, Nixes Mate Review,* and *Bending Genres Journal.* Additionally, she has been published in numerous anthologies including *Bending Genres Anthology, 56 Days of August: An Anthology of Postcards, Driftfish: A Zoomorphic Anthology, Hospital Drive Anthology: University of Virginia,* and *Blue*

Heron Review. A book of her poems, *Wind Eyes*, is forthcoming from MadHat Press Autumn 2024.

Linda Kleinbub is the Founding Editor of Pink Trees Press, curator of Fahrenheit Open Mic, contributing editor at Girls Write Now, and co-founder of Pen Pal Poets. She's the author of *Cover Charge* (Autonomedia, 2022) and *Appear to Dance* (Pink Trees Press, 2024.) She's co-editor of the *Silver-Tongued Devil Anthology* (Pink Trees Press, 2020.) Linda was one of six local poets invited to read at the Americas Poetry Festival of New York 2021. She earned her Master of Fine Art in Creative Writing from The New School. She's published in *Best American Poetry*, the *Brooklyn Rail*, *The Observer*, *Sensitive Skin Magazine*, *LiveMag!* and many anthologies.

Sandra Kleven is publisher at Cirque Press, Anchorage, Alaska, home to the literary journal *Cirque*, now in its 13th year. Since an expansion beyond the journal in 2018, thirty-five books have been published. Kleven's writing has been printed in various journals including *AQR*, *Stoneboat*, *Oklahoma Review*, and *F Magazine*. Her first book of creative writing, *Defiance Street: Poems and Other Writing*, came out in 2010. Kleven is the author of *Holy Land*, a collection of writing about the issues found in rural Alaska (AQR, 2005), and two children's books aimed at abuse prevention, *The Right Touch* and *Talk About Touch*. Her interest in the literary history of Seattle led to the creation of the film *To the Moon: A Tribute to Theodore Roethke* in 2008 (find it on YouTube). Kleven has an MSW degree from Eastern Washington University and an MFA in Creative Writing from the University of Alaska/Anchorage. Kleven coordinates Poetry Parley, an event held monthly in Anchorage, AK. She's been awarded two Celebration Foundation grants for creative work and an Emmy for an earlier film project. Born and raised in the State of Washington, Kleven has spent most of the last 40 years working with Alaska's tribal villages as a clinical social worker.

Elizabeth Morse values the quirky, the darkly humorous. She is hard-wired to be a night-owl and writes exclusively after 9 p.m. Her work has been published in literary magazines such as *Ginosko*, *The*

Raven's Perch, and *Kestrel*. Her poetry chapbook *The Color Between the Hours* is forthcoming from Finishing Line Press in late 2023. She was a finalist in the Blue Light Press full-length poetry collection contest and has her MFA from Brooklyn College.

Andrea Nicki (aka Austėja Nagrodski) is a poet, writer, educator, visual artist, and expressive dancer based in Vancouver, Canada. Her first poetry book, *Welcoming*, was published by Inanna Press, her second, *Noble Orphan*, by Demeter Press, and her third, *You Can Make Your Own Rose*, by Mago Books. Her imagistic poetry explores complex social issues, like child welfare, family, sexual violence, cultural dislocation and immigration, and capitalism and social isolation. Her poetry is also joyful and includes eco-spiritual writing and writing that celebrates community. She is currently working on poems about her paternal Lithuanian heritage and Lithuanian history, culture, and paganism. She has a PhD in philosophy, with a specialization in ethics, from Queen's University in Ontario, Canada, and held a postdoctoral fellowship in bioethics, trauma, and narrative writing at the University of Minnesota. She is also working on a multidisciplinary book, under contract with Rowman and Littlefield Publishers, which draws on narrative poetry, poetry therapy, bioethics, feminist philosophy, social work, and dance studies, which includes an exploration and analysis of her own poetry. She teaches undergraduate courses in humanities and academic writing.

Sue Oringel is a poet and writer, a teacher of creative writing, and a psychologist in private practice in New York's Capital District. Her first full-length book of poetry, *Carnevale*, was published by David Robert Books in 2023, a chapbook of poetry, *My Coney Island*, was published by Finishing Line Press in June 2019, and a short story, "The Relative Truth," in *Tiferet Journal*, Spring/Summer 2021. A graduate of the Warren Wilson MFA program, she is published in various journals such as *Blueline*, *The Maryland Poetry Review*, *The Paterson Review*, and *The National Council of Teachers of English Journal*. She also served as co-translator for a collection of Latin American poetry, *Messengers of Rain*, published by Groundwoods Press in

2002 and 2011. Fellowships and awards include Individual Artist award from the Albany Schenectady League of Arts, a fellowship from the Vermont Studio Center, and an SOS award sponsored by NYSCA. She taught creative writing at Hudson Valley Community College from 2004 to 2017.

lisa roma, aka ElectrikGoddess, is a poet, photographer, calligrapher, painter, songstress, who croons her tunes to trees and starry nights. She writes haikus and free style eco-poetry, shaping Nature's soul into lovesongs. lisa roma is also a writer, editor, and interfaith minister. She sings Brazilian-influenced jazz and classics, American songbook, showtunes, pop and folk music. Her original song recordings can be listened to online. As founder-director of Creative Women's Network, she offers literary, design and promo services. She is founder-director of The Half Moon Theatre Co., a virtual performance vehicle for musical theatre. lisa does freelance editing, and sometimes book design and layout for psychoanalysts and researchers at IP Books. Her artwork, poetry and photography have appeared in *Medicinal Purposes, The Eve's Legacy Trilogy, RiverRun, Nine Lives: Wings Lift* (RenkuNINE), *PoeticJava Publishing,* and *Modern Drummer* magazine [feature on jazz drummer/bandleader Drori Mondlak]. She is currently reproducing her combined poetry and photography books, *Emerging from Limbo* and *Haikuisized,* as one. lisa also has a children's book, memoir, novel, screenplay, and musical theatre project, in various stages of development. She attended The Brooklyn Museum Art School, taught Language Arts, and holds a BFA in Creative Writing/Poetry from Brooklyn College. lisa received a first prize Donald Whiteside poetry award and several honorary mentions.

Claire Donohue Roof is an assistant professor of English at Ivy Tech Community College. She has been the editor of the *Ivy Quill,* a creative writing and arts journal, for eight volumes. She attended IU at Bloomington for her Bachelors' Degree, attended graduate courses in creative writing at the University of Houston, and attained her Masters' Degree in English Education at the University of Saint

Joseph in West Hartford, Connecticut. She has been published in the *Common Ground Review*, the Cincinnati Poets Collective, *DeepLiterary Journal*, *Pirene's Fountain*, *Flint Hills Review*, and will have poems in the upcoming *Aoelian Harp*, Volume 9. She studies with the writer Larissa Shmailo in her writers' workshop, and studies also with Megan Merchant, poet and editor.

Audrey Roth is the author of *Arms Akimbo: A Journey of Healing*, a child sexual abuse memoir too raw to be considered poetry. She uses her writing to build strength and resilience, both her own and her readers'. Audrey recently won a baseball poetry contest run by the National Baseball Poetry Festival. Audrey has read her poetry at the New York City Poetry Festival and at other venues in NYC and Boston. She is currently working on a prose memoir of her healing, a chapbook of baseball poems, and a collection of spiritual poems, with the support of her lifelong friend and mentor, Larissa Shmailo. Audrey is an inveterate (ex-pat) New Yorker, as well as a financial adviser, a recovering lawyer, and a poet. She is also a mom, a lesbian, a Jew, a feminist, and a singer. She is the proud mama of her daughter, Phoebe, the loving, out-and-proud spouse of her wife, Deb, and the proud personal scratching post for Hercules (her cat).

Cynthia Lee Steele serves as Associate Editor for *Cirque*, wife of Bill, mom of Shania and Donte, and dog whisperer. She has an MA in English and a BA in Journalism and has published news stories statewide. Her new work appears in *Cirque*; *Pensive: A Global Journal of Spirituality & the Arts*; *The Blue Mountain Review*, and in the *Anthology on Domestic Abuse*: "When Home is Not Safe." Chapters from her forthcoming nonfiction book *Thirty Before Thirteen* have been published in *Cirque* and other journals.

Meg Tuite is author of a collection of three of her books (*Domestic Apparitions*, *Bound By Blue*, and *Her Skin is a Costume*) *Three By Tuite* (Cowboy Jamboree, 2023), *White Van* (Unlikely Books, 2022), *Meet My Haze* (Big Table Publishing, 2018), *Bound By Blue*, (Sententia Books, 2013), won the Twin Antlers Collaborative Poetry award from Artistically Declined Press for her poetry collection *Bare*

Bulbs Swinging (2013), *Grace Notes* (Unknown Press, 2014), a novel-in-stories, *Domestic Apparition* (San Francisco Bay Press, 2011), as well as five chapbooks of short fiction, flash, poetic prose, and multi-genre. She teaches workshops and online classes through Bending Genres and is an associate editor at *Narrative Magazine*. Her work has been published in over 600 literary magazines and over fifteen anthologies including *Choose Wisely: 35 Women Up To No Good*. She has been nominated over 20 times for the Pushcart Prize, won first and second place in *Prick of the Spindle* contests, five-time finalist at *Glimmer Train*, finalist of the Gertrude Stein award and 3rd prize in the Bristol Short Story Contest. She is also the editor of eight anthologies. She is included in the *Best Small Fictions* of 2021 and *Wigleaf*'s Top 50 stories 2022 and 2023.

www.ingramcontent.com/pod-product-compliance
Lightning Source LLC
Chambersburg PA
CBHW031958010726
47493CB00007B/2250